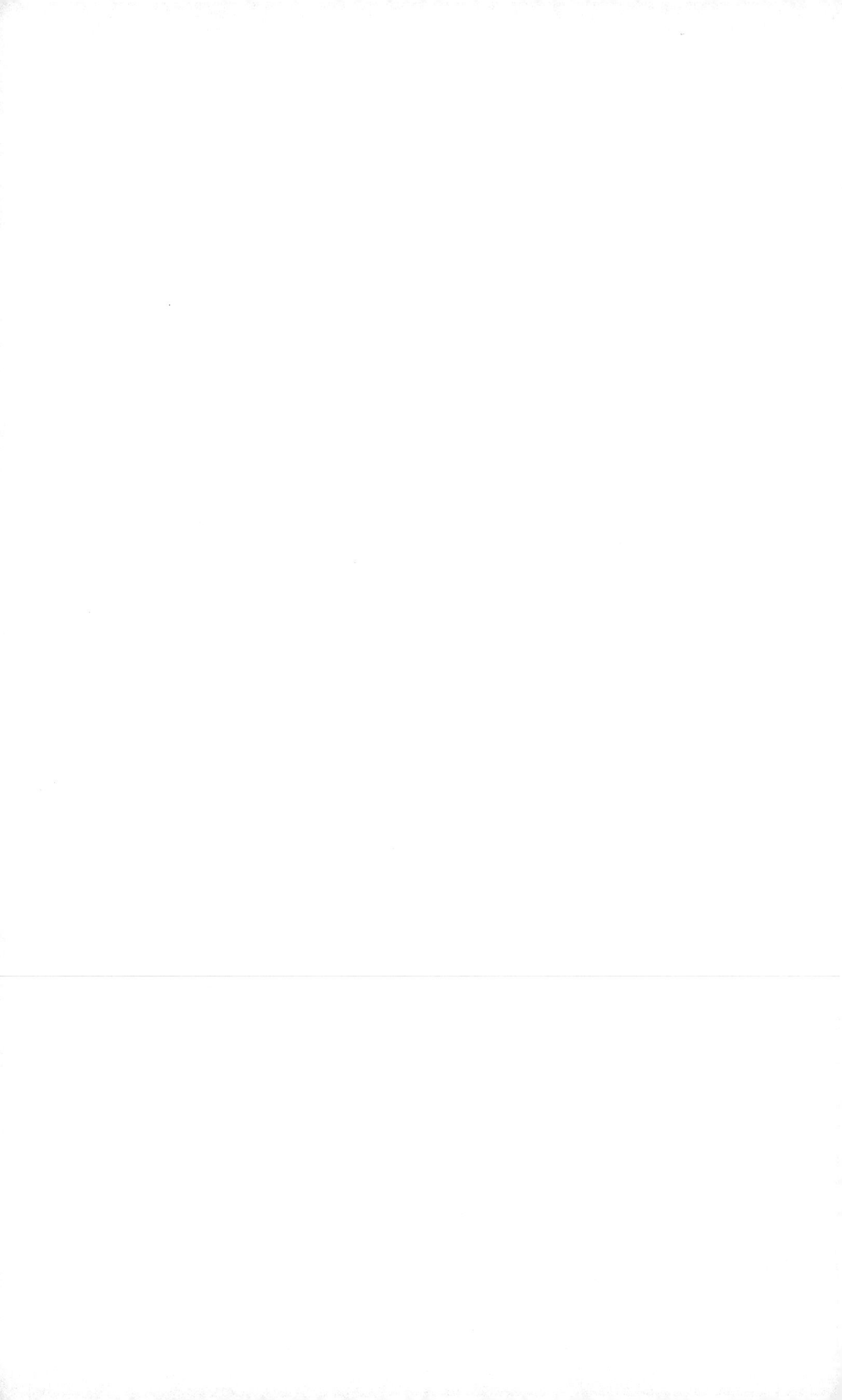

TWO WOMEN CONQUER THE WEST
(AND THEIR HEARTS)

CHARLIE STEEL
Tale-Weaver Extraordinaire

ILLUSTRATED BY
BARABASH SVIATOSLAV

TWO WOMEN CONQUER THE WEST
(AND THEIR HEARTS)

CHARLIE STEEL
Tale-Weaver Extraordinaire

ILLUSTRATED BY
BARABASH SVIATOSLAV

CONDOR PUBLISHING, INC.
Lincoln, Michigan

TWO WOMEN CONQUER THE WEST (AND THEIR HEARTS)

by Charlie Steel

December 2024

AI (artificial intelligence) was not used in the writing or creation of this book.

*Cover and Illustrations by Barabash Sviatoslav
(All illustrations property of Condor Publishing, Inc.)

Library of Congress Control Number: 2024952714

This is a work of fiction. Names, characters, places, and incidents either are the product of the author's imagination or are used fictitiously, and any resemblance to persons, living or dead, business establishments or locations is entirely coincidental.

ISBN-13: 978-1-931079-66-2

Condor Publishing, Inc.
PO Box 39
123 S. Barlow Road
Lincoln, MI 48742
www. condorpublishinginc. com

Printed in the United States of America

This book is dedicated to all strong women.

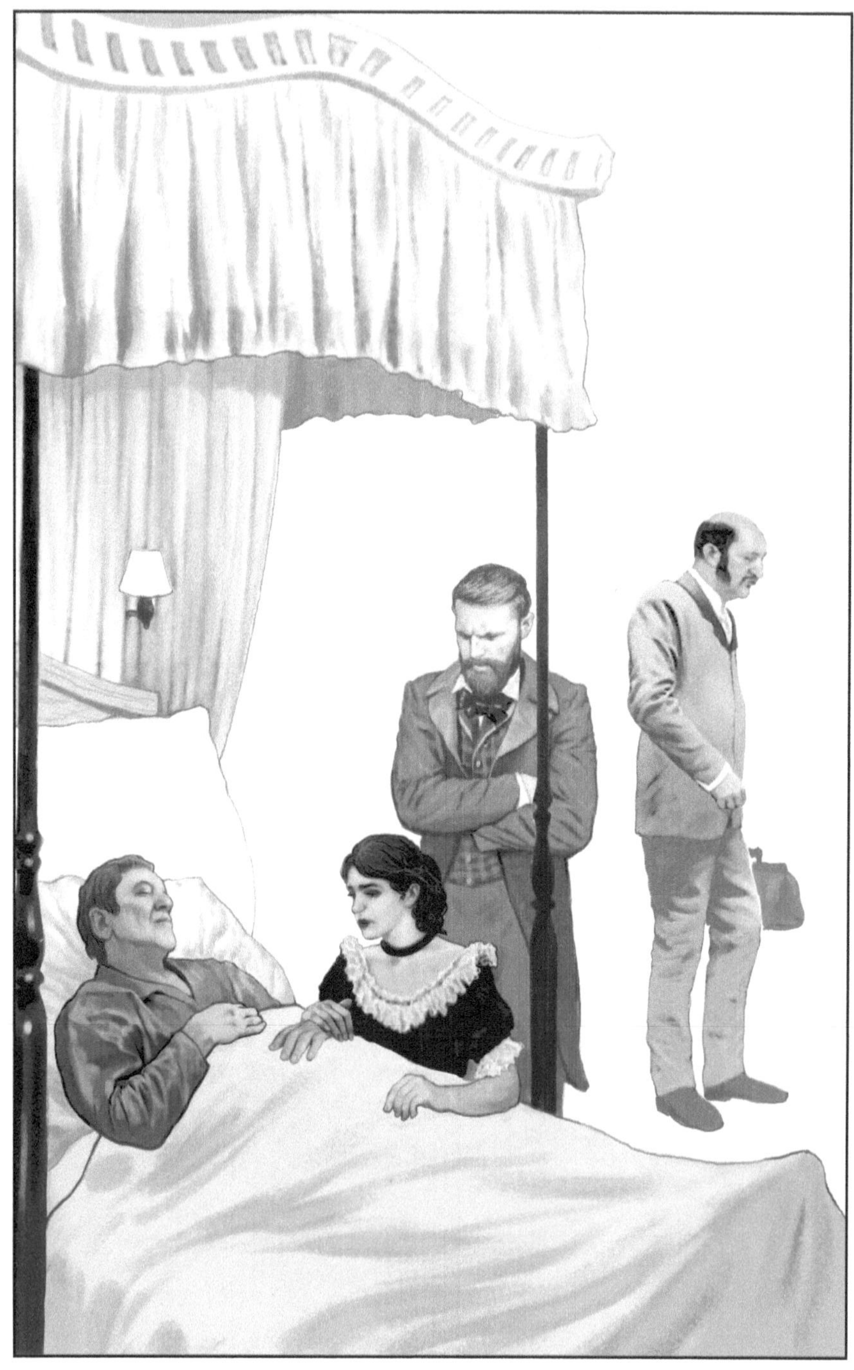

CHAPTER 1

"Here's some food, Father. It's chicken soup, and I made it myself."

"My love, how incredibly kind of you, but I've told you before, that's why we pay the cook."

"But Father, Mother taught me how to make this…"

"You and I just can't get away without mentioning her name at least ten times a day, can we?"

"I'm so sorry, I…"

"Don't make it worse by apologizing. That's the trouble. I thought I was strong and never realized how much I relied on her. And…it's the little things, Miss Lizzy Burnett...it's all the little things I'm missing about your mother that are so hard to endure."

"Perhaps you would feel better if you go upstairs and lie down," said Elizabeth.

"No, I can't go up there right now. I just can't bear it."

"Please, Father, you must eat something. It's been days and you hardly…"

"No, I won't eat, and I won't go upstairs. But you must know by now, I won't last long anyway. The doctor was here early this morning, and he says the cancer…"

"Oh, Father."

"You must know everything is in order, but just for peace of mind, I called our lawyer, and he will be here this afternoon. We're going over the Will, and I'm leaving everything to you except for a pension for the cook, butler, and maid. They've been with us so long and have become part of the family. I hope you won't object…"

"Whatever you have done, I will support…"

"That's my little Lizzy."

"Father, I am twenty-six years old and not so little."

"No, I suppose not. If only you had married."

"Father!"

"Well, it's true. Then I wouldn't worry so. It's the one thing that keeps me…"

"You and Mother brought me up well. I will be fine."

"But still, my dear, with all the money I'm leaving you, I worry that some man will try to take advantage."

"You needn't worry. No man has yet and never will."

"All those eligible young men you've met and you never favored…"

"No, Father. And you know why. Not one of them has been like you. I won't marry until…"

"I met and married your mother before I made my millions. In fact, it was because of her guidance that I did. But you, my dear, you have money, and you'll never know if the man you meet is marrying for love or for…"

"You and I have discussed this before. I promise you, the man I meet and fall in love with will never know that…"

"But, Lizzy, it was just in jest, a humorous conversation at dinner. My brother Henry started it; Mother and I joined in. You mean to really go through with such a scheme he suggested?"

"I do. The men I've met here in New York don't measure up, Father. You know that. Behind a veneer of manners and good education, every one of them looks at a woman's bank account before her figure and mind. And, in that order. They use women to get ahead, and I won't have anything to do with…"

"Perhaps your standards are too high, my dear."

"It was you and Mother who gave them to me."

"Yes, Lizzy, perhaps we were a bit zealous in your upbringing."

"No, you were overly protective."

"Perhaps, but don't you forget, both of us genuinely found you to be a most remarkable daughter. You have been the joy of our lives."

"I have known that all my life. But please, as a favor, eat some of my soup. I spent hours…"

"You would find some way to coerce me…the thought of food is nauseating…but…very well. Before I do, promise me that when I am gone, you will consult with Uncle Henry before implementing some mad scheme. Thank goodness Henry has a good head on his shoulders and will see that you come to no…"

"I promise, Father. Now eat your soup."

"Don't forget, Elizabeth, you are a young lovely woman, and when I am gone, a rich one. You will be quite vulnerable to all sorts of mischief."

"Yes, Father, I promise you I will consult with Uncle Henry and will be very careful."

CHAPTER 2

Mrs. Blanche Graham opened her bedroom door. Before her stood her landlord, Mr. Guiltner.

"You have been in my home for two months now, Blanche."

"Yes, Mr. Guiltner."

"My wife has gone to buy groceries, and the children are out. Perhaps now you will show me how you appreciate the spare room."

"Sir, I work hard to pay for that room. The agreement was ten dollars a month. I have purchased my own food. There is no cause for you to be familiar."

"No cause? I'll show you how to appreciate your betters…"

The front door of the high-ceiling apartment opened, and Mrs. Guiltner came in carrying a sack.

She was tired and went to a chair and sat down, holding the small sack of groceries on her lap. She stared at the floor, completely oblivious to the people before her.

"What are you doing home so early?" exclaimed her husband.

Mrs. Guiltner raised her head and, for the first time, noticed her man in his undershirt and pants, standing in front of her boarder's bedroom door.

"If you must know, Mister High and Mighty, my purse had less money than I put in it, and I couldn't buy much. You've taken money out of it again, Franklin."

"It's just like you to blame me, woman! Why don't you point the finger at one of the children instead of me all the time!"

"Because, Franklin, the children don't drink, and I normally hide my purse, and you're the only one who knows where. But when you…say…what's going on here?"

"Shut up, woman!"

"Franklin, if you do something to scare our boarder and lose the ten dollars, I'll…"

"You'll what?"

"I swear, husband, one day you'll go too far and…"

"Hush up, woman, and fix dinner. I'm hungry."

"Did he try something?" Mrs. Guiltner asked the young woman?

"He was starting to," Blanche replied. "I lost my husband, but I haven't lost my dignity, Mrs. Guiltner. I'll be looking for another place to stay as soon as…"

"Please, Blanche, don't do that. We...I...don't I provide a perfectly good room? Don't me and the children leave you to your privacy? My husband won't bother you no more. I promise. Ain't that right, Franklin?"

"Awe, you both can go where's it's hot," replied Guiltner, grabbing a shirt and beginning to button it up.

"Where are you going?" asked his wife.

"Both of you are enough to drive a man to drink," he replied as he walked unsteadily to the door.

"Haven't you spent and drunk enough for one day?" asked Mrs. Guiltner.

"Not nearly enough!" shouted her husband.

He opened the door and disappeared, slamming it violently behind him.

The door banged, failed to catch, and then swung open. Mrs. Guiltner closed it.

"I'm sorry, Blanche, but when my husband drinks, he becomes a completely wild man."

"That's what I'm afraid of."

"Please don't go," pleaded the landlady. "You won't find no better room to rent. Not for the money. Some places just ain't fit for a single woman like yourself."

"I'm sorry to say it, but I'm afraid of your husband, Mrs. Guiltner. Drunk or sober."

"It's no different anywhere you go, Mrs. Blanche Graham. Men are a burden for certain to bear."

"If I may, it wasn't like that with my Jack. He was a kind, sweet, hard-working man. When the accident at the factory took him, it was almost as if a part of myself died…"

"Yeah? If you say so. All I know is the men and women in this apartment building. You can hear them arguing day and night. It's no different than what's on my hands, and I think that death has colored your vision and your memory. If it wasn't for the money he earns, I swear, most times I wish that some accident would…"

"Mrs. Guiltner!" exclaimed Blanche.

"It's the God's truth! Well, if you're going, I can't stop you. But be sure to pay up for the week when you do leave!"

“I will, and it’s to you I will be giving the money from now on until I find another place to live.”

“Just try to find such a nice place as this, Mrs. Graham!”

“Mrs. Guiltner, I’ll be going to buy a few things for my supper now.”

“You do that!”

Blanche locked her bedroom door, walked through the apartment into the hallway, and closed the main door behind her. Immediately, the powerful odor of cooked cabbage, along with the smell of sweat, dirty clothes, and stale tobacco smoke, struck her nose. Blanche made her way along the scarred wooden floors and dim littered hallway to the squeaking stairs that led seven stories down.

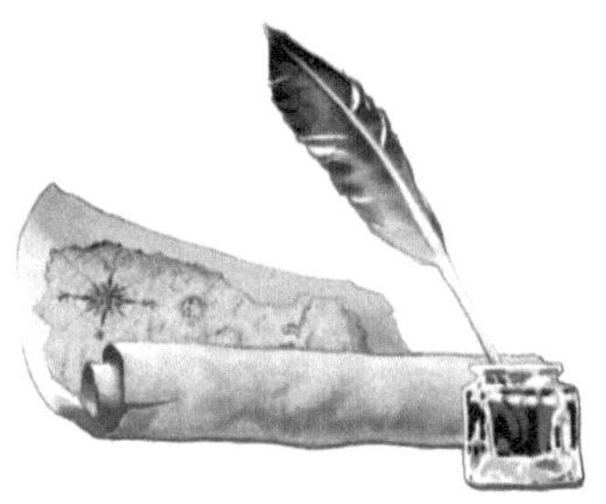

CHAPTER 3

"Miss Burnett, the doctor is asking for you," said the maid, looking very old and tired.

"Thank you, Dora," replied Elizabeth, who had been pacing in the living room.

Elizabeth raced upstairs to her father's room. Uncle Henry and the doctor were standing at the end of the bed. The doctor came up to her and whispered in her ear.

"He has only a few moments."

Elizabeth knelt beside her father and took his hand. He looked ghostly white.

"It's all right, my dear," said her father. "The flesh weakens and must come to an end. I am confident that our souls will live on. So please don't be unhappy. Just think, I will be with her again."

"Yes, Father," whispered Elizabeth, tears streaming down her cheeks.

"Lizzy, my dear girl, don't cry. You have so many fond memories of our times together."

"But, Father, I love you and will miss you so."

"I am sure you will," her father said. His breathing was weak and shallow. "Be grateful for me that I can throw off this broken body."

"Yes, Father."

"There now, that's better. Take my hand, dear, I am having trouble…"

"But I am..."

In that instant, her father closed his eyes, and his last breath left him in a long, slow sigh. Elizabeth began to cry in earnest. Long heaving sobs escaped her, and she remained on her knees, still holding her dead father's hand.

Uncle Henry, fighting his own grief came forward and put his hand on Elizabeth's shoulder. Then, he and the doctor helped her stand up and led her to her own room.

"We are both going to miss him, Elizabeth, but he is no longer suffering," said Uncle Henry. "I will sit here beside you for a while if you like."

Too full of grief, Elizabeth did not respond.

"I'm afraid," whispered the doctor, "even though she knew this was coming, this will be very hard on her, she being so close. I will leave medicine for her to take if you think it necessary."

"No," replied Henry Barnett. "She will take it hard, but Elizabeth is a strong-minded and healthy girl. I don't think medicine of any kind will help her right now—she needs time to work through it. As soon after the funeral as possible, I will be sending her west. I think action is what the girl needs. She's been cooped up too long in this house dealing with her mother's death and now her father's. What she needs is change."

"Perhaps you're right," replied the doctor.

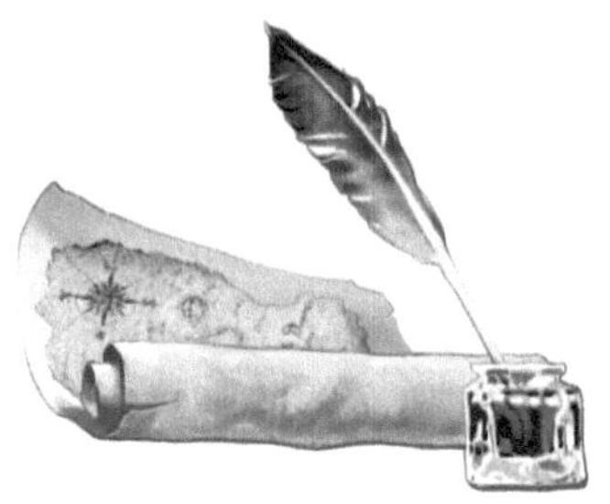

CHAPTER 4

After losing her husband, Blanche Graham had a difficult time. They had been married two years, planned on raising a family, and were very happy together. When he died, they had saved their money and were ready to purchase a modest brownstone. Jack Graham had a good factory job. He had worked his way up to supervisor when there was an explosion; several men were killed or injured. Afterwards, there were bills and debt to be paid, and what savings they had went quickly. Blanche's parents were dead, as were her siblings, many close relatives had passed away, and she was left destitute. Having to fend for herself, she finally took up a job scrubbing on her hands and knees as a cleaning lady for government buildings. She received the lowest form of pay. Blanche had become nearly homeless when she found a single room for rent. One she could barely afford and still be able to buy food.

Daily, Blanche looked for discarded newspapers in the trash and desperately looked for better job opportunities. Repeatedly, she spent what little money she saved to buy passage to job interviews. She failed to secure better employment as a housemaid despite dozens of attempts. Now, after Mr. Guiltner's drunken behavior, she was forced to look for a new room to rent. So far, the better ones were more than the ten dollars she paid monthly to the Guiltners.

Tired, Blanche purchased a half loaf of bread, cheese, and milk and carried her items back to her building. She dreaded climbing the seven flights of stairs to her rented room. Using her key, she was met inside the main building door by Mr. Guiltner, and it was evident he had been drinking.

"Well!" exclaimed the drunken man. "If it ain't our fancy boarder. Come here and give your landlord a kiss. Haw! Haw!"

Blanche moved quickly away before he could approach her. She turned in the dim foyer and forced the heavy door back open. Tired beyond measure, the woman ran up the street not knowing where she could go. It was already dark, and she had spent the last of her money on another failed interview.

Mr. Guiltner followed.

"Where are you going, you stuck-up hussy?" he yelled. "You women are all the same!"

Blanche continued to run, desperate not to lose her footing. The only place she could think to go was the library. There were benches outside to sleep on, but a dangerous place at night. Then, there were the police who arrested vagrants.

CHAPTER 5

"It was a very special funeral, wasn't it, Lizzy?"

"Yes, Uncle Henry, it was. Father was well liked."

"Did you notice the people in back, a strange and poorly dressed group…"

"Father helped those of various stations in life," responded Elizabeth. "Several of them spoke to me afterward."

"Yes, and your mother gave him heck for it," said Henry.

"Mother was wrong to scold him. His kindness and generosity are among the many things I loved about him."

"Me too, my dear, me too. I learned a lot from my brother. Now tell me, Lizzy, what do you have in mind?"

"Nothing. I'm far too upset to want to do much of anything. I shall go back to the house and go through Father's things. Arrange his papers in the library, and…"

"The lawyer is coming this afternoon to read the Will."

"Father already told me he would be leaving a pension for the maid, butler, and the cook. He is right to do so, they have been a part of the family for a very long time. I hope he left them adequate…"

"He did. Far more generous then what I would have been," explained Uncle Henry. "You see, your father and I discussed everything before…"

"I bet he left you instructions about me," replied Elizabeth.

"He did. Now, in a few short hours you are going to become a rich young lady, a most eligible young woman, perhaps the most eligible in all of New York City. No doubt that will produce a plethora of suitors. They will be coming out of the woodwork. Tell me how you are going to defend…"

"I won't answer the door or the mail. Not to one single individual."

"Not even to that Leonard Newton?"

"Especially not him."

"Then tell me, do you intend to be an old maid all your life?"

"Uncle Henry, my father just died. It is impolite and far too soon to be thinking…"

"On the contrary, my dear, this is *precisely* the time to start that little adventure we spoke of."

"You can't be serious."

"I am. The maid, butler, and cook are old. Dora will be retiring with the funds your father left her. She'll be most comfortable, indeed. She has provided for your needs most of your life."

"Yes, I shall miss Dora. That goes for Davis, the butler, and the cook."

"May I suggest first that you advertise…no… leave it to me. I'll advertise for a new maid and traveling companion, and you and I shall interview prospects together."

"But Uncle Henry, I am so…it's far too soon…I just couldn't…"

"Now hush, Lizzy," replied her uncle. "Leave it to me to arrange. You are going on a trip and a grand adventure. In this way, I follow your father's instructions to look after your happiness."

***

Leonard Newton attended the funeral. Lizzy had been preoccupied and dismissed his friendly handshake as if he were among the many laborers or poor people who came to thank her. It was an affront. How dare she ignore him? After all, hadn't her father shown him favor? Hadn't Mr. Burnett encouraged him to court her? Elizabeth had gone out with him several times and then abruptly declined his further interest. No other woman had been so cold to his advances. But then, no other woman was as rich as Elizabeth Burnett.

You won't get rid of me so easily, thought Leonard. *I'll be seeing you again, you rare rich beauty. You can count on that.*

The handsome young man watched from a distance. Elizabeth displayed a shapely leg and ankle as she stepped up and entered her uncle's carriage. Leonard actually licked his lips at the sudden, unanticipated sight.

***

"Elizabeth, there is just one more interview," explained Henry. "This woman comes highly recommended. She says she worked for the

Leonard Newton family in the past. You can look at her references and the families she…"

"If she worked for the Newton family, I don't want her."

"Excuse me," interrupted a slim, well-dressed young woman. "Your butler showed me in, and I couldn't help but overhear. I know Leonard Newton and his parents. They are people of upper society, and although they seem to be going through some financial difficulty at the moment, they are of the most respectable…"

"I'm sorry," replied Elizabeth, "but it's out of the question. For personal reasons if no other. Uncle Henry will escort you out."

"But…"

"I'm sorry, young lady, your name again?" asked Henry.

"I am Amelia Mitchell, and I come with the highest references if you would only…"

"Miss Mitchell, my niece has no intention of causing offense, but it is, after all, up to her what companion she chooses. If she feels uncomfortable that you know the Newton family, then I must respect her wishes. Please let me apologize for the inconvenience of your trip here. May I pay for your carriage? It's the very least…"

"I don't even get an interview?"

"I'm sorry," said Elizabeth. "I don't mean to be rude, but I have my reasons."

Henry guided Miss Mitchell to the front door and gave the butler money.

"Davis, give this to the carriage driver and let him keep the change," said Henry.

He turned to the young woman, "I wish you well in your future endeavors."

"Leonard said your family was aloof," said Miss Mitchell. "Now I believe every word…"

Henry watched the butler lead the upset young woman down the stairs, and he closed the door mid-sentence.

"I'm sorry, Lizzy," said her uncle. "If I had known beforehand, I would have…"

"That is a young woman I certainly would never have picked in any case, Uncle Henry."

"Now, what do we do? Of all the candidates we interviewed, not one came close. Did they?"

"None."

"I see this is going to be more difficult than what I thought," commented Henry. "I can't imagine I volunteered to help you find a maid and traveling companion. All those women were simply dreadful."

At this last comment, a loud knock came at the main door. Whoever it was must have gotten around the butler, for he would usually answer the summons. Before the uncle could react, Elizabeth opened the large, heavy door. Before them stood a slight woman in unremarkable dress. She looked terribly strained and distressed despite an effort to put on her best smile. Nevertheless, she was quite attractive, and there was an honest and likable intensity about her.

"Yes?" asked Elizabeth.

"I saw the ad in the paper for a maid and traveling companion? I hope I'm not too late. My name is Blanche Graham, and I came in answer to your ad."

"Miss Graham," said Henry. "The advertisement specifically calls for references and an appointment before responding. And how did you get past the butler?"

"He was helping a lady in a carriage. I scooted up the steps. I so need this position. I apologize, but I work during the day, came home late, and just found the ad. I didn't have time to respond. Please give me an interview. That is if it is not too late. I've traveled and walked such a long way, and..."

The butler had performed his duty and returned to the entrance. He stood behind Miss Graham and listened politely.

"Davis?" said Elizabeth. "Will you take the lady's wrap and bag?"

The butler did as requested.

"Will you follow me, Miss Graham?" said Elizabeth Burnett.

"I'm sorry, it's Mrs. Graham," replied Blanche. "I'm a widow."

After working all day, Blanche was tired, and she tripped and nearly fell. Following behind, Davis, the butler, caught her arm and steadied the woman. Uncle Henry and Elizabeth noted the incident and Henry shook his head vigorously at Lizzy. At the same time he gave her a questioning look. Elizabeth nodded her head at him and smiled mischievously.

There was a long walk through the foyer, the large living room, and to a library in the rear of the house. The young woman stared uncomfortably around her all along the way and stumbled once more before catching her balance.

"Will you please take a chair?" asked Elizabeth, pointing to a high-backed, richly embroidered Victorian.

Blanche Graham sat down abruptly and completely exhausted. Wild-eyed, she looked over the vast shelves filled with leather-bound books, the high ceiling, and the large lavish chandelier. Overwhelmed by the luxury of the house and extremely agitated, she closed her eyes tightly and tried to calm herself. Uncle Henry and Elizabeth did not overlook any of this. Both remained standing and exchanged questioning looks.

"Mrs. Graham," began Elizabeth. "You seem to be somewhat distressed. Is there anything I can bring you to drink?"

"Please, call me Blanche. Why yes, I am quite thirsty…oh my…it's not appropriate for you to be offering me…"

Uncle Henry crossed the room to where a tray with a pitcher of water and glasses stood. He took a glass, poured it nearly full and brought it to the young woman. Blanche took it, smiled weakly, and drank thirstily. She nearly drained the glass and then looked for a place to set it. Uncle Henry took it from her and returned it to the tray. The uncle and Elizabeth remained standing.

"Thank you so much for the water." Uncomfortable, Blanche looked once again around the room and then focused on the two people before her. "You must think I look dreadful. I know I do, but please understand, I worked all day, and then I caught an omnibus, which is a great distance from where I live. I had trouble with the address and mistakenly got off at the wrong stop. Knowing the interviews ended at six, I ran the rest of the way. I apologize for…"

"Tell me Blanche," interrupted Elizabeth, "what made you make so much effort to come here."

"I'm sorry, I know I must look terribly desperate…but…you see…I am."

"Take your time," said Uncle Henry, now becoming interested and somewhat solicitous to this unusual woman.

"I don't know where to begin," replied Blanche.

"How about stating your references and qualifications," replied Elizabeth.

"I don't have any…I mean in the usual sense. You see, up until a few months ago, I was married, and my husband…he died. It was an accident. It wasn't expected. We were in the process of buying a home…and…when he was taken, I lost it. My family passed away a few years ago and all my close relatives and there was no…"

"Go on," said Uncle Henry.

"Oh," said Blanche, stomping one foot. "I do want to be proper. You asked about experience. All my life, I have worked in one manner or another for my mother and father and cared for my brother and younger sister. I cooked and cleaned and cared for my husband…"

"What are you doing now for employment?" asked Elizabeth.

"I clean," said Blanche, looking up at her prospective employer.

"For a family?" asked Uncle Henry, attempting to smile at the increasingly distressed young woman.

"No, for the City of New York. You see, I am a cleaning lady. After my husband died it was all I could find."

"Mrs. Graham," said Uncle Henry. "Would you excuse us for a moment? There is something I must talk to Miss Burnett about."

Henry took Elizabeth's arm and gently guided her into her father's old office and closed the door.

"It's impossible," said Uncle Henry. "I know she seems like a remarkable and likable young woman, but we know absolutely nothing about her. Imagine, a cleaning lady, a scrub woman."

"Uncle, you know very well that it's through no fault of her own. She lost her husband and her family and is doing the best she can. I couldn't find a sweeter maid or traveling companion if I interviewed half the women in New York City."

"If we can believe her," replied the uncle.

"Did you just really say that? Just imagine what she has gone through…is going through."

"But we just can't hire a stranger, a cleaning lady off the streets."

"Why not? We would be helping her and she would be helping me. I like her, Uncle Henry. I believe every word she said. Don't you?"

The older man raised his hands and shrugged his shoulders. Staring at Elizabeth and seeing her broad smile, the uncle succumbed and smiled back.

"She is a sweet, adorable, little thing, isn't she?" said Uncle Henry.

"Come, let's go back and ask her to speak a little more about herself," said Elizabeth. "She's so endearing and kind. I bet you a glass of blackberry brandy that every word she speaks is God's truth."

"I'm not disputing one word she says, nor am I taking up that bet. But when she leaves, I'll do the pouring."

"Uncle," said Elizabeth. "We may not be able to let the poor thing leave. Who knows what dreadful circumstances might befall her. Besides, I bet she doesn't have a penny to get back home in any case."

"You mean we ask her to stay?"

"What else do you think we should do?"

Again, Uncle Henry smiled warmly, shrugged his shoulders, and helplessly raised two hands. But this time, he also shook his head in astonished disbelief.

The two Burnetts listened to Blanche for some time. The more they questioned, the more assured they became of the truth of this tragic woman's circumstances. An hour later, they hired Blanche Graham and, through polite persuasion, convinced her to stay. The next day, Elizabeth took her new companion shopping and ordered her a bevy of suitable shoes and clothing, most to be completed by tailors.

"After all, Blanche," said Miss Burnett. "It is part of your job. My maid and traveling companion must be suitably clothed."

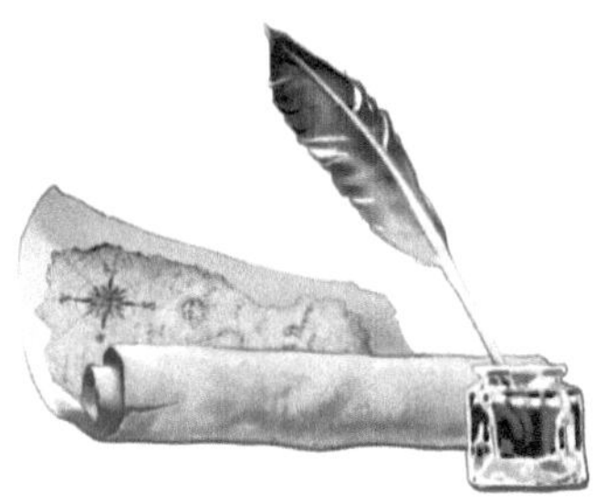

CHAPTER 6

"Lizzy and Blanche, I must tell you that I have been planning this little adventure for some time," said Henry. "Ever since it came up in a dinner conversation over two years ago. You remember, Lizzy, when your father was upset about you breaking off contact with Leonard Newton? You told your father that he was only after your money and that he was a complete cad."

"I remember," said Elizabeth.

"Then you observed that *all* the men you were meeting were cads and were only interested in your wealth rather than who you were as a person."

"Yes? What about it?" replied Elizabeth.

"Then you started to say you wished you could meet men who didn't know you were rich. If it could occur, you would be sure the man you married loved you for who you were, not for your money."

"Uncle Henry," said Elizabeth. "We've been over this conversation many times. Please tell me, what is your point?"

"Don't be so impatient, my dear," replied Henry. "The point is…ever since that conversation… which I might say, I instantly understood your dilemma….I thought about how you could pretend to be average, rather than rich, and safely meet a good man."

"Yes, Uncle, but that hardly…"

"Don't you see? I want to explain to you and Blanche what this is all about. After all, Blanche will not only be your helper but also your companion, confidant, and protector."

"Uncle, please." Elizabeth protested.

"Stop interrupting, Lizzy," said Henry. "Now, where was I? Oh yes, Blanche, I'm counting on you that on this trip…this grand adventure…that you will stay by Elizabeth's side and protect her?"

"Of course I will," replied Blanche.

"Then good," said Henry, grinning broadly. "Now I will explain my plans."

"Uncle," said Lizzy. "Sometimes you are so darn exasperating."

"Tell me what you think after I tell you. You know that your father was against this little scheme from the start. Although, at the time, before I began to take it seriously, he and your mother joked about you dressing up as a pauper and working as a cleaning lady or some such thing. Err…no offense, Blanche."

"None taken," replied Mrs. Graham.

"First, my utmost concern for you both, is your safety. Your father, God rest his soul, would never forgive me if you came to any kind of harm. So…"

"Uncle!" exclaimed Elizabeth, actually stomping her foot in consternation.

Henry laughed.

"That won't help you," he said and laughed once more. "Your safety, ladies…that's the ticket, and now let me explain. I have spent nearly two years planning this. Lizzy, from now on your name will be Elizabeth Graham. If Blanche has no objection."

"None that I can think of," replied Blanche hesitantly.

"Good. Elizabeth, you are to pretend to be cousins with Blanche. Both of you have come into an inheritance; an uncle, me, purchased a little cattle spread near Denver and died before ever having seen the ranch. According to my agent, the place is fifteen thousand acres, with…"

"Uncle," interrupted Elizabeth. "That hardly seems like a poor man's ranch…"

"Young woman!" replied Henry. "Sometimes you are impossible! First, you complain because I'm too wordy, and then you complain when I am actually explaining…anyway…where was I? Oh yes, out West, I'm told a really good ranch has fifty thousand acres or more, with additional open graze. You see, they need lots of land because it's so dry. It takes forty acres just to feed one steer. So a fifteen thousand acre spread isn't really that big in the West. And your place has about four hundred breeder cattle that produce about four hundred calves a year, and many don't survive. Also, there are forty horses, and various other animals. The ranch employs ten cowboys plus the cook and foreman. There's a bunkhouse, a barn, and a modest little house.

The place earns less than ten thousand a year, but expenses run close to six thousand. That includes thirty a month per ranch hand, and the ranch expenses. In fact, with the mortgage, the place barely made a profit. That's how I was able to buy the ranch. The previous owner was disgusted that he wasn't getting anywhere and…"

"Uncle?" said Elizabeth. "Must I spend my time on a ranch and perhaps meet and marry a cowboy? At thirty a month?"

"Elizabeth!" laughed Henry. "I thought you wanted to meet and marry a real man?"

"Sometimes, Uncle, your humor goes too far."

"Lizzy," replied Henry. "Don't you see? You need a cover. You need to prove you're not rich, you need another name, which Blanche provides, and you need a place to live and stay while you're looking for the right man."

"And what will I find on a ranch?"

"Denver is not far away. After the Great Conflict the railroads crossed the Missouri and built the Transcontinental Railroad. Spurs began to be laid all over the West, and in 1880, the first one reached Denver. This is 1888, my dear, and many educated men have gone west to seek their fortunes. There are mining engineers, bankers, mine owners, politicians, and, in fact, any type of man you can find here in New York, you can find out West. Better men, I say, men who have brawn and are willing to take risks, seek adventure and fortune."

"I didn't think of it that way," said Elizabeth. "All I thought of was…"

"Dirty, uncouth men and smelly cowhands?"

"Uncle Henry, you know very well that I don't hold my head above any person, but at the same time, I don't think an uneducated man would…"

"Never mind," said Henry. "I was just playing. I am sure Blanche would agree with me that out West, you have the opportunity to find a decent, hardworking fellow who is seeking an equally honest, hardworking woman to share a life and family with."

"I do," said Blanche.

"Then, there is no further argument about the ability to find future prospects?"

"Well…," Elizabeth said skeptically, "I'm unconvinced. I'll have to find out for myself. And if it doesn't work out, I'm leaving."

"Good, then…," replied Henry. "Think broadly, both of you. Just imagine. Wide open skies, snow-capped mountains, fresh, clean air, miles and miles of open prairie, horseback riding, all kinds of animals, and occasionally a wild gun-toting cowboy. The West is not completely tamed. Not yet."

"Are you going with us?" asked Elizabeth.

"I would if I could, but I can't. I purchased a factory and it's taking a loss. A rather large and substantial factory, and if I don't clean up the mess and turn a profit within the next year, I myself will need a loan from you. And, given the circumstances and your father's trust, I'm afraid that's something I couldn't do."

"But Uncle, I would do anything to help you," stated Elizabeth quite soberly.

Henry Burnett smiled.

"I know you would, Lizzy. But rest assured, I have your father's blood in me and I'll turn that factory around and make a profit. But right now, we have that ranch to talk about. It's in an assumed name of mine, and maybe someday, who knows, we can turn that into a money-making affair."

"You are sending Elizabeth and me to the ranch by ourselves?" asked Blanche.

"Of course not," replied Henry. "Like I said, I have been thinking and planning this adventure for Lizzy for over two years. What I have done is hire a bodyguard. Not just any bodyguard, George Temple, a former sergeant of mine from the war. We fought for the Union, and Blanche, you don't know, I was a Major…"

"Uncle...," said Elizabeth.

"Yes, Lizzy, I know, I ramble. George will teach you both how to clean, load, and shoot various firearms."

Henry opened a lacquered box and inside was a matching set of derringers. One at a time he handed the little pistols to each woman.

"If you want to know, this is a new Remington Model 95 Double Derringer in .41 rimfire, with over and under barrels. Both of you will carry this on you from the start, and so long as you are out West, you will *never* go anywhere without it. Not even to the privy. They have rattlesnakes you know."

With that, Henry began to laugh, and it took some time before he recovered. Seeing Elizabeth's raised eyebrow and wrinkled forehead, he sobered and continued the conversation.

"You will meet George Temple this afternoon, and he will take you to a firing range and begin instruction on these pistols. In addition, I have requested him to show you how to fire a Winchester model 1873, .44-40 centerfire cartridge. If you don't know what that means, I assure you, by the time George finishes, you will know how to disassemble, assemble, clean, and accurately fire these weapons. His instructions are not to let you leave for the West until you do. And this, dear ladies, is more than most men learn."

Chapter 6

"George Temple is to watch over us, Uncle?"

"He is, at all times. You are going to be followed and watched from a distance by George. I hired him away from the New York City Police Department, where he worked his way up to becoming a Captain. He is now retired with a pension. George is competent and you will find ladies, a man not to be trifled with. He saved my life in the war more than once. I have every confidence in him."

"It sounds like you have thought this out very thoroughly," stated Elizabeth.

"I have," replied Henry.

"But how do we explain who George Temple is once we reach the ranch?" asked Blanche.

"You are to say he is your uncle's friend and came along as a protector of you two young ladies. And that's not far off from the truth. In case you're wondering about the need for money, he will handle any emergencies."

"Is that all?" asked Elizabeth.

"There is another last thing I forgot to mention. To carry this off, both of you will have a brand new set of clothing to match your station in life. When you travel, you will be two poor cousins wearing practical gray dresses. When you arrive at the ranch, you will adopt the clothing of the country and wear the Western dresses and clothes of your peers. George Temple will do the same."

Elizabeth suddenly smiled and then laughed.

"Uncle, I bet you wish you were going on this trip with us."

"I planned on it, and then the unexpected mess with the factory. But I assure the two of you that as soon as that is cleared up, in a year at the most, I will be joining you as another long-lost uncle."

"I can't believe," said Elizabeth, "that I am actually going along with this!"

***

"You fool, Amelia!" said Leonard Newton. "Why did you ever say that you worked for us?"

"How did I know that she hated you?" replied Amelia Mitchell. "Lenny, this time you were too closed-mouthed. Whatever scheme you were planning to use me for, backfired. In a way, I am relieved. I sure wouldn't want to work for that arrogant, self-willed Elizabeth. From what I hear, all the Burnett's are an independent, hard-nosed bunch who never…"

"Enough, cousin Amelia," shouted Leonard. "And don't ever call me Lenny again! You're no good to me now; you can go."

"And the money you promised me?"

Leonard fumbled with a money pouch and handed her three twenty-dollar gold pieces.

"You promised me a hundred dollars, cousin."

"Go on, you're not worth even that."

"I hope you do get that girl," replied Amelia. "The two of you deserve each other. And cousin, if you are successful, mark my words, you'll get more than you bargained for."

Leonard watched Amelia walk to the front door and exit.

Good riddance! thought Leonard. *Too bad she had to be let into this. Even one person in the family who knows of my interest in Elizabeth Burnett is one person too many. If Amelia ever opens her mouth...*

Leonard Newton paced the front room of the large house.

Father had to make that bad investment. The fool spent my inheritance. We'll lose even this house if I don't find money soon. I'll just have to think up some other plan. Elizabeth hired a traveling companion for a reason. I need to find out where she's going so I can plan what to do next.

***

Uncle Henry stood on the train platform with Blanche, Elizabeth, and George Temple. The three travelers were plainly dressed, and nothing about them indicated wealth. Henry was pleased.

"Elizabeth," began her uncle. "George assures me the two of you learned how to handle those weapons and that both of you can shoot quite well."

"Yes," replied Elizabeth. "And we enjoyed learning."

"I'm glad. I would never want you to be a victim, Lizzy. I don't want you harmed by anyone. It would have been wrong to send you without you having some kind of self-defense."

"I always felt that whatever a man can do, I can do better, or at least equally well," replied Elizabeth.

"I never told you this Lizzy, and now I will. At sixty, I'm an old bachelor and accustomed to it. But when I was young and working with your father, I met your mother at the same time he did. Your father was the better man and he won her heart. I fell in love with your mother as well. I never told a soul, but after meeting her, there could never be another woman for me. That's why I planned this trip to try to give you the happiness you seek. Elizabeth,

I always thought of you as the daughter I never had. Go now and find the man of your heart. Find and marry him and raise a family. Have a bunch of children that I can claim as nieces and nephews and pamper to no end."

"I love you very much, Uncle Henry," said Elizabeth, her eyes shiny with tears.

"And I you," replied Henry. "All of you go and have a grand adventure. Be safe, and remember that I will join you as soon as possible."

From behind a bench and partition on the platform stood a man who listened to every word of the exchange. When the three persons boarded the train, and the uncle on the platform finally departed, the stranger came out from his hiding place and went up to the ticket window.

"I'm afraid I'm too late. Two women in gray dresses and a man boarded the train. I had a special package for them. My boss will be upset. Could you tell me their destination?"

"You mean the two pretty women and the stern-looking man?"

"They're the ones."

"I'm not supposed to give out information about…"

The surveillance man gave the ticket agent a twenty-dollar gold piece.

"Denver," whispered the ticket taker. "Their passage is all the way through to Denver."

***

The two men met on a street corner.

"You fool!" shouted Leonard Newton. "I told you to follow them!"

"All the way to Denver?"

"Yes!"

"I'll remind you, sir, that you gave me forty dollars in expenses, and twenty of that went to bribe the ticket taker at the train depot. I did not have the money to buy a train ticket and go all the way to Denver and return."

"Then tell me who Elizabeth Burnett was traveling with and what they took with them."

The man took out a notebook and looked at what he had written.

"There was a maid named Blanche Graham. There was a man with them, who looked like a policeman. Probably a bodyguard. I could not get his name. They each carried a carpetbag, traveling light, and the two women wore gray dresses, and the man was plainly dressed. They looked like any third-class travelers heading west."

"You're fired!" said Leonard.

"My pay, sir."

Leonard dropped several coins into the outstretched hand of the private detective.

"You're fifty dollars short, Mr. Newton."

"Do half a job, get half the pay."

"It's not smart to stiff a person such as myself," said the fired agent.

From his clothing, he produced a pistol and plunged the barrel into Newton's belly. Leonard gasped, bent over, and then quickly backed up. He began to raise a hand to his suit coat and was stopped by the pointed revolver.

"Not wise, Mr. Newton. I performed my job as you asked. I'm a professional, sir, and if you value your life, you will hand over the other fifty."

Reluctantly, Leonard Newton cautiously reached in his jacket pocket and scooped up a change purse. He opened it and counted out the amount in gold coins.

The hired man took the money, turned, and put several passersby between himself and Newton.

Leonard placed his hand on the butt of his pistol, but it was too late to fire.

That fool detective, thought Leonard. *The trains are packed with travelers heading west. Denver will be crowded with miners and foreigners looking for work. Elizabeth could be anywhere and hard to find. If she dressed as a common traveler, it must mean she has some sort of scheme or plan. Perhaps she changed her name. That little minx, she'll not get away from me so easily. It doesn't matter how long it takes; I'll find her and make her regret snubbing me. It doesn't matter if I am out of money; I'll find more. I'll sell what I've got left or steal it and go after her myself. There isn't a woman on earth who rejects me, Leonard Newton. I swear on my life that she will pay.*

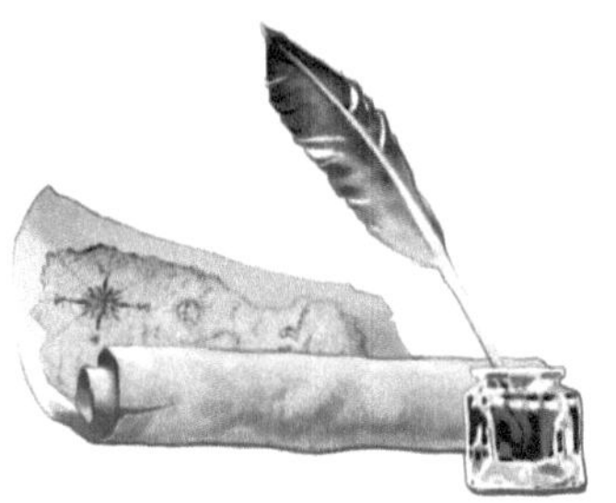

CHAPTER 7

The train car was a long, flat-roofed wooden box with a stove and convenience at opposite ends. The car was crowded with all types of passengers. Most were foreigners who spoke German, Italian, and other more obscure languages. Many of the roughly garbed men were Irish. Elizabeth and Blanche sat together, and George Temple sat several rows back. There were a myriad of odors aboard the train and not all of them were human. At times, the wind blew the acrid smell of smoke down upon the train cars, and some of it entered through cracks and burned the eyes of the passengers. Beneath the conversation of many tongues, the train swayed and jerked and emitted a constant clacking of steel wheels over steel tracks.

"I think it's going to be a long and difficult trip," said Elizabeth.

Blanche, who had never traveled anywhere and had never been on a train, was next to the window, staring out at the flickering images. She turned wide-eyed, looked at her new employer, smiled, and shook her head.

"Oh no," said Blanche, "I think it's going to be grand."

Elizabeth smiled at Blanche and then both of them had the same secret thought. *Who was protecting whom?*

They rode for hours. From time to time, the train would make stops, and passengers would board; very few departed, and the train became more crowded. Most travelers brought something to eat, and those who didn't purchased from enterprising newsboys who sold items of food at train depots along the way. There were newspapers, fruit, lollipops, cigars, soap, towels, washing tins, coffee, tea, sugar, and air tights of hash, bacon, and beans. All the while, Blanche continued to stare out the window at the countryside and constantly commented to Lizzy about the things she saw. She was amazed at the farms, the well-plowed fields, the endless acres of growing crops. The vastness of the farmland continued on and on across the country. The further west they traveled, the more open the land became. The sky loomed larger in the dry air and became a huge half-round dome of blue. Distance expanded and they could see for miles and miles.

"Do you think we will see Indians and buffalo?" asked Blanche in sincere innocence.

"We'll certainly see cowboys," whispered Elizabeth. "From what I read, the buffalo are nearly all gone, and those Indians who survived are on reservations."

"What a pity," replied Blanche.

"Yes, it is," responded Elizabeth in a soft voice. "The West is nearly tamed now."

It was almost impossible to sleep sitting up, and they were both very tired. After traveling all day and all night, the two ladies attempted to wash with soap from a tin basin and complete their ablutions. In the toilet they removed their gray dresses and put on more colorful ones. It was a difficult process given the crowded space and the swaying of the train.

Elizabeth wanted to stretch her legs and, against the wishes of George Temple, Blanche and Lizzy stepped down from the stopped train onto a station platform. They paced to the end of the passenger cars. Returning, Elizabeth noted three cars stuffed with passengers. One car contained only immigrant men; from open windows, many poorly dressed males stared at the two women. A last car contained Chinese, and a third immigrant car held men, women, and children. Blanche had purchased an apple, and she was about to take a bite when the thin arm of a boy reached pleadingly.

"The poor thing," said Blanche, handing the child the apple.

There was a cry from the train car, and hands grabbed and stole the fruit from the boy. Both Lizzy and Blanche watched in dismay.

"Ma'am," said a conductor. "You're making matters worse. I recommend you go back to your car. The train will be departing shortly."

"But those poor children are starving," replied Elizabeth. "Can't you at least give them something to eat?"

"They paid immigrant passage," said the conductor.

"What does that mean?"

"These immigrants took it upon themselves to come west. Ma' am, if you want the truth of it, their troubles are just beginning. Wait until they get to the mining camps; then, they'll really know hardship."

"I want you to gather the children outside the car," said Elizabeth. "So their parents can't steal the apples I'm going to purchase for each and every one."

"Can't allow that, Ma' am. There's no time, and besides those families are packed in like sardines. It would cause all kinds of havoc and delay…"

"Blanche," said Elizabeth. "Hurry! Run and get one of those newsboys with a cart, and we'll buy all the fruit they have."

Blanche did as she was told and returned with a boy and a loaded contrivance. From somewhere in her clothing, Elizabeth pulled out a twenty-dollar coin.

"How many apples will this buy?" asked Elizabeth, handing the coin to the newsboy.

"Every apple I got!" beamed the lad at the sight of the coin.

"Then let the three of us start handing up the fruit to the children."

Blanche grabbed several apples and began placing them into eager, hungry-looking children's hands. To Blanche's dismay, male adults grabbed the apples from the children and disappeared in the crowded train car.

"Children only!" shouted an angry Elizabeth to the crowded windows filled with the extended arms of men, women, and children."

"I say," shouted the conductor. "Stop this!"

"Having trouble, Ma'am?" asked a man with sombrero, boots, and at his waist a wide belt, holster and pistol.

It was to Blanche the Westerner spoke.

"These children are hungry. The conductor is trying to stop us and the parents are stealing the apples. All we're trying to do is…"

The cowboy grabbed his revolver and pulling it, fired a shot into the air.

"All right!" shouted the cowboy. "You in the car! Let your children be!"

For emphasis, the Westerner fired two more shots in the air. Adults disappeared from the windows, and dozens and dozens of small faces, arms, and hands appeared extended through the open train car windows. The cowboy put away his pistol, and together, the newsboy, Blanche, Elizabeth, and the Westerner handed out apples until there was no more fruit left. Still, hungry faces and hands extended at the window.

Chapter 7

"What will I do?" asked Elizabeth.

"I reckon you've done all you could, Ma'am," replied the cowboy.

Elizabeth glanced at the cart and noted lollipops and cans of airtights. Searching in her clothing, Lizzy produced two more twenty-dollar gold pieces.

"Will this pay for the rest of your goods?"

"It sure will!" shouted the youth.

"You're holding up the train!" exclaimed the conductor.

The Westerner eyed the trainman, and the conductor frowned but said no more. Once again, the party of four began handing items to eager hands. It took only a few moments for the occupants of all sizes to gather lollipops, tins of beans, and hash.

"Lady," said the newsboy. "You bought the whole cart; we might as well give it all to them."

The youth took up a final box containing tins of tea, coffee, and cigars and handed it through the open window to be caught by several men.

"All aboard!" shouted the conductor.

Elizabeth and Blanche ran for their train car, and the cowboy followed them. They boarded, and the train started with a lurch before both women could reach their seats. The Westerner was behind Blanche, and when she fell backward, the cowboy caught her.

"Excuse me," cried Blanche, and then turned red-faced before getting her balance and reaching her bench.

The only empty seat left in the car was beside George Temple. The cowboy sat down, eyes upon the two women several rows before him. George Temple kept his external look of indifference when the Westerner turned and nodded his head at him. But inwardly, the bodyguard was seething.

How could Elizabeth pretend to be poor when she so flagrantly handed out money for those children? he thought. *Attracting everyone's attention on the train was NOT part of the plan. These two attractive women will be much harder to look after than I imagined.*

Blanche turned several times to get a glimpse of the cowboy. The Westerner smiled, put three fingers to the brim of his sombrero, and Blanche beamed back.

"Blanche," said Elizabeth. "You are making a spectacle of yourself. Whatever will that man think?"

"Oh," exclaimed Blanche. "Isn't he handsome?"

"Yes, he is," replied Elizabeth, attempting to keep her composure but eventually grinning back at her companion. "He's tall, handsome, and quick of action. If it wasn't for him those children…"

"Yes," replied Blanche. "So gallant! A real man when we needed him the most. Oh, I wonder what his name is."

"Blanche! You just met him, and you know nothing about him."

"I know he is all those things you said. And, if I have my way, I *will* get to know him. He's the most exciting man I've met since my husband…"

Blanche bowed her head, and Elizabeth saw that her friend's eyes watered.

"I know it's wrong of me, but I can't help myself, Elizabeth. I have no right to be enjoying this trip when I am working for you or…to be so happy."

"You're not wrong, Blanche," replied Elizabeth. "Why shouldn't you speak to that young man? After all, he helped us just at the right moment."

"But how will I talk to him?" asked Blanche.

"If you promise to quit looking back," said Elizabeth. "In a little while I'll turn and call him to come up the aisle. I'll thank him for his assistance, and then perhaps the two of you will start chatting.

I'll make an excuse to get up, and you can invite him to sit down. The two of you can be together for a time and talk. I'll go back and sit with George. He won't like it, but…"

"Oh, Lizzy," said Blanche. "You are the best boss…"

"Cousin?"

"Cousin…a girl ever had!" exclaimed Blanche.

Both young women looked at each other and giggled like two little girls.

"I promise not to look back," said Blanche. "But please don't wait too long. He might be getting off at the next stop."

Ten minutes passed, and Blanche became increasingly fidgety. Finally, Elizabeth turned and nodded to the watching cowboy and smiled. She raised her hand and crooked a finger. Instantly, the Westerner arose and came forward. Elizabeth Burnett thanked the young man for his assistance and then asked to be excused. She rose and walked down the swaying aisle to plop down beside George Temple.

Not one to lose his composure easily, George raised an eyebrow and, still pretending not to know the young lady, whispered to her.

"You're not supposed to know me."

"Perhaps not, George," said Elizabeth, "but circumstances call for desperate measures."

"Very well, Ma'am," said George in a loud voice. "You're most welcome to sit here."

Elizabeth smiled broadly at the many passengers who continued to notice the two unusually attractive women aboard the train car.

"What on earth was that display back at the last stop?" whispered the bodyguard.

"There was a car full of children. They were hungry; I just couldn't let them starve."

"You could have, but you didn't," whispered George. "Did you have to let that cowboy use his pistol? Now the entire train will never forget the three of you."

"No, perhaps not. But I would never have been able to live with myself if I hadn't helped, at least a little. I do hope it did those poor children some good."

"My job is to see to your safety," whispered George. "From now on, will the two of you, please refrain from making a show of yourself. And… why is Blanche talking to that Westerner?"

"If I have to explain that," smiled Elizabeth to her bodyguard, "then Uncle Henry hired the wrong man."

"Oh, understand all right," clipped George. "But it doesn't mean I have to like it. You two young ladies aren't sticking to the plan. Remember, you are supposed to be two poor cousins…"

"Sometimes, my dear sir," replied Elizabeth, "life doesn't unfold according to plans!"

George gave the young lady one of his disdainful glares, folded his arms, and then looked away in disgust. Elizabeth noted the man's actions and then turned her attention to Blanche and the cowboy. The two of them were in active conversation, and to the low hum of many voices, the clacking of wheels, and the swaying of the train, Elizabeth sat and watched. She had a little pocket watch she pulled from her reticule and noted the time. The decorum would be fifteen minutes. Elizabeth would give them thirty, and then she smiled broadly and sat back. She relaxed as best she could on the train car bench. Beside her, the surly bodyguard continued to pretend he did not know her. Alone with her thoughts, Elizabeth smiled, wondering what else would transpire on this trip to the West. Like her uncle predicted, this was beginning to already be a grand adventure.

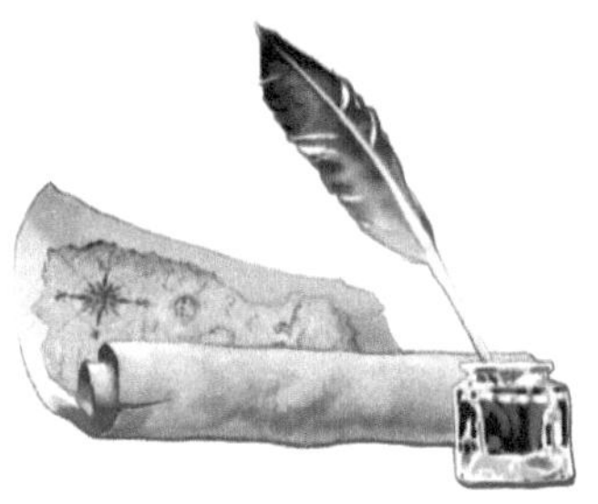

CHAPTER 8

"You're late, Son," said Paul Oliver Newton. "In fact, I can't recall any important meeting in the last few years where you haven't been."

"Did you bring me to this isolated spot to lecture me, Father, or because you were afraid I would make a scene?"

"At least you are astute and no dummy," replied the father. "Yes, I called you here for both reasons and more. Shall we stroll? I am finding that a long walk each day does my constitution good."

The father set out on a leisurely walk along the path leading into Central Park, putting the silver-handled cane he carried to good use.

"I wonder at your energy, given that you lost the family fortune," said Leonard.

"There it is, on the tip of your tongue and in the opening conversation. *Money.* It is the only subject I have heard you speak of since you were a young lad. I am afraid I spoiled you, Leonard, for the fortune you speak of is one I made through hard work and self-control. Two virtues I am afraid you are sadly lacking."

"How can you lecture me when you so foolishly lost our money, Father? We're poor now. How can you even hold your head up? Don't you hate the ground you walk on, now that everything is lost? The house, the carriages, the servants, the money…"

"Leonard, you forget. It was money I made and money I lost. I became rich once, and perhaps I can come close to it again before I die. If you had talked to me about it, I could have explained that the Newtons can still hold their heads up. Leonard, I want you to know this…I made a bad business deal…but I made good on all my debts. Before I lost everything, I sold my investments and the house and paid off every penny I owed. In the process I managed to retain enough for your mother and me to live on. At least, until I get started again. I kept my business contacts in good standing. Because I acted reputably, I have obtained a vice presidency in a bank. I have already started the position and…"

"I was told, Father, that you could have kept most of your money if you just refused to pay off your debt. No law prevented you…"

"Leonard!" exclaimed his father. "My honor and my reputation were at stake. Something I value more highly than even money. There were many others involved. Men and their families would have suffered. Don't you see…"

"All I see is a foolish old man who lost his…"

"Son!" exclaimed Paul Newton. "Not only have I spoiled you about money, but also moral values."

The two had stopped to argue along the walk. Now Leonard moved forward, and the father hurried to catch up. There were many people in the park, some taking walks, others lying on blankets on the lawn. There were foreigners, oddly dressed, well-dressed personages, and families with children enjoying the ambiance of the greenery set down among the crowded buildings of New York City.

"Leonard!" said the father, now walking briskly. "This conversation is long overdue. Now slow down a bit and hear me out."

Leonard Newton responded by walking even faster. He turned and looked at his father with intense dislike.

"You shouldn't hate me, but you do, don't you, Son? It makes me sad. I gave you everything, and I see now that it was the wrong thing to do. How many times have I bailed you out? Even in your youth, you coveted money in all the wrong ways. I remember those boys' parents. I had to compensate financially for the bullying and extortion schemes you played upon them. How many schools were you kicked out of? How many jobs have I obtained for you and you lost because of your unsavory practices? And that embezzlement charge took no end of finagling to get you free. And now, right at this moment, you have no visible means of support, but yet here you are dressed as a gentleman and…"

"Enough of the lectures, I didn't come here for that!"

"Why did you meet me, Leonard?" asked the father. "Was it because I might still have something left of my fortune that you…"

"I hoped."

"I thought so. Son, if you don't reform your ways I am certain you will come to a bad end. I beg of you to listen to me. Stop whatever crooked scheme you're planning and become an honest hardworking man. I called you here today to offer you a good opportunity."

"I don't want it," replied Leonard Newton. "I won't grub for money or take other people's orders; I'm above…"

"No, Son, you might think you are, but you are not. You are just a man; without integrity, you become something other than a Newton. My father and his father were hardworking honest men. They came from England to start a new life and each generation of us has…"

"Yes, I've heard this a million times and don't want to hear more."

The father came to an empty park bench and abruptly sat down.

"I can't go any further," said Paul Newton. "My heart is not what it used to be. Now hear me out, Son. I am offering you a job as an accountant in a bank. You have the education and you always had a good head for figures and numbers. You are more than qualified. This is a good opportunity with above-average pay. In a few years, if you do well, there is promotion, and if you remain steady, perhaps one day a…"

"No. I won't take some boring low-paying job in a bank."

"Son, whatever you have planned, I beg you to take this job. The society you used to run with knows you haven't a penny to your name. How you have been living with the funds cut off, I just cannot imagine. And, I have heard some rather distasteful rumors about your behavior with several young eligible women and…"

"What, Father?" challenged the son. "What have you heard?"

"I won't go into that. All I ask is that you change your ways before it is too late, and take the job I have secured for you."

"No, I won't." replied the son. "I have other plans. I'm going west if you must know. I have a business deal I'm working on."

"I hope that's true, Son. I hope with all my heart that it is an honest undertaking. No matter what you think, Leonard, you are my son, and I do care what happens to you."

"Please, Father, at least spare any sentiment. It's too late for that."

"I am afraid that I have raised you rather badly."

"Oh please," exclaimed the younger man.

"Whatever you're planning to do, I hope it is an ethical scheme. I've been out West, and you are going to find that the men out there are decisive and quick to action."

"Goodbye, Father," said Leonard Newton.

Before Paul Newton could reply, his son had turned and was already several paces up the walk. A family group was strolling towards Leonard, and the father watched his son discourteously walk briskly toward and through them, causing children and a parent to step aside. Mr. Newton shook his head at his son's behavior and, at that moment, knew that he had not changed but, in fact, had become worse. A certainty came to the older man that he would never see his son again. The thought saddened him, but mostly, it was regret that he had raised a boy who had somehow, long ago, taken the wrong path in life.

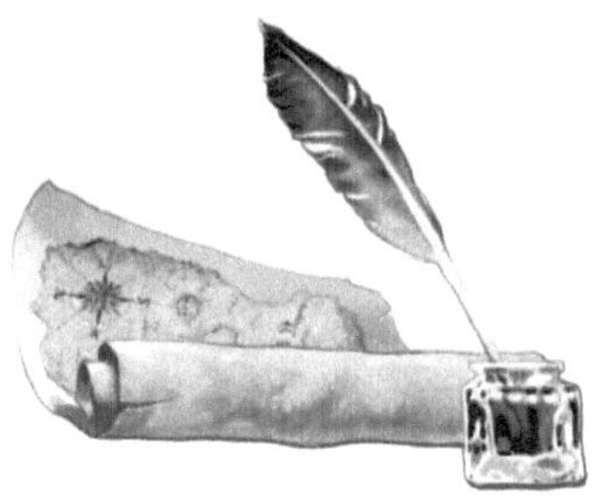

CHAPTER 9

"Miss Elizabeth," began the cowboy, standing in the aisle, sweeping the sombrero off his head and holding it nervously in his hands. "Miss Blanche has told me about you. Let me introduce myself. I'm Lawrence Roth; my friends call me Larry. I'm in the cattle business. My father sent me and his cowhands to sell the fall steers. Now that it's done, I'm meeting him at the next stop in Wichita, and we're gonna…"

"You're in the cattle business, Mister Roth?" interrupted Elizabeth, smiling at the obvious discomfiture of the Westerner.

"Yes Ma'am, I mean Miss Elizabeth. That's what I was telling Blanche, I mean Miss Blanche, that I know a lot about horses and raising steers, and she told me that you're on your way to take over a ranch. Since I spent all my life ranching I offered to look your spread over and make suggestions. She said I had to ask…"

Behind the cowboy, Elizabeth could see Blanche making faces and vigorously nodding her head up and down. She was very obviously mouthing the word *"yes."*

"We know nothing about you, Mister Roth, and I mean…we…couldn't just hire anyone."

"Not asking for money, just offering my advice. To tell the truth, it will give me an excuse to come visit Miss Blanche."

"I see," said Elizabeth hesitantly.

"I understand you're real keerful for your cousin," interjected Larry. "I'm not just some cowpoke off the range, Ma'am. I'm sort of a foreman for Benny, I mean my father. I got sort of an interest and a percentage in the herd. It's not exactly like I'm some broken-down thirty-a-month hand. You see, when I was little, Benny Roth adopted me, and I've been workin' my way up ever since and…"

Larry Roth had shifted his hat to his right hand, and when he spoke about an interest in the herd, he patted his belly. Elizabeth looked at it and noted a large and unnatural bulge. The unusual gesture revealed what was obviously a money belt around the waist of the tall, lanky man.

"Are you eventually looking for a foreman's job?" asked Elizabeth.

Larry Roth smiled broadly, revealing a row of snow-white teeth.

"No Ma'am, I was just asking permission to come and visit, and maybe I could help out some. Maybe I could meet the ranch hands. Perhaps look over the water, grass, and the hosses and steers and give advice if'n they or you might be wantin' some. This being the West and all, I wouldn't put my nose where it wouldn't be…"

"What would your father say?"

"Dad? He'd be some plumb put out, but when I explain to him about Blanche, I mean…"

Larry turned beet red. He was drawn short on what he had just revealed and could go no further.

"What you are asking me for Mister Roth, is permission to look over our ranch and give advice for free. An excuse to come to visit and get to know my cousin Blanche a bit better?"

"Yessum, Ma'am," replied Larry Roth, suddenly plopping his wide chapeau upon his head. "That's it exactly."

"Did Blanche tell you that we haven't seen the ranch and that we know very little about it?"

"No, Miss Elizabeth. I guess we didn't have time to get around to that. But if I could be of any help, I sure would be pleased to…"

"Suppose you give us a month to get settled," replied Elizabeth. "You and Blanche can write by general delivery, and she can send directions. Do you think that would be…"

Larry Roth smiled broadly, grabbed Elizabeth's right hand, and shook it vigorously, interrupting her speech.

"Why that would be just fine, Miss Elizabeth. Just grand! You won't regret this, I promise I…"

"Suppose you go back to your seat now, Mister Roth," whispered Elizabeth. "I'm afraid we're creating a bit of a scene. Write down an address for Miss Blanche Graham to write to, and you can give it to her before you depart."

"I'll do that, and thank you, Miss Elizabeth," replied the tall cowboy. Turning, he went down the aisle to sit once again beside the stern George Temple.

"Say, fella," began the cowboy. "You wouldn't happen to have something to write with, on you?"

Staring sourly, George took a pad and pencil from his jacket and handed it to the Westerner.

"Mighty obliged," said the cowboy.

When the train stopped at the Wichita depot, Larry Roth sauntered up the aisle and once again removed his hat before the two young women.

"Miss Blanche, Miss Elizabeth, I reckon when one most needs time, there's never enough of it. Here's the address to write to…and…Blanche," said the cowboy, reaching across and taking her hand. "Now, when those other cowboys start to flirtin', you just tell them you already have a feller who's comin' to visit. Now take this. This here is a twenty-dollar gold piece with part of a bullet. Some cattle rustler nearly did me in. It's my lucky piece, and I never go nowhere without it. I will give it to you for safekeeping. It's to let you know that when that month is up, I'll be on your doorstep for sure. I'll be lookin' forward to that letter and don't you be forgettin' me. For I sure won't be forgettin' you."

Before Blanche or Lizzy could say anything, the tall cowboy made a low bow, smiled, and, placing his wide hat upon his head, walked up the aisle and off the train.

"Oh!" exclaimed Blanche, holding the paper with the address and the dented gold coin in her hand. "Isn't he just the sweetest, kindest…"

"Reminds me of a large boy who hasn't quite…"

"If you say anything bad about him, Lizzy, I'll just be heartbroken…"

"What I'm thinkin'," imitated Elizabeth. "Is that boy will be just plumb proud to come visit you."

"How will I ever survive a whole month?" asked Blanche, without realizing that she said it out loud.

Elizabeth grabbed the coin from Blanche and studied it. After a moment Blanche seized it back and held it tightly in her hand. Together they sat and Elizabeth watched her companion become lost in deep reverie. Up the train car, passengers departed. Two cowboys boarded, laughing loudly. It took only a moment for Lizzy to realize that they were very intoxicated. The train started with a lurch; this time, the sound of motion and clacking of steel wheels was welcome over the loud voices of the two drunken men.

It took some time before the armed drunks noted the pretty women. One of the men whooped when he saw them.

"Well, looky there, Frank," exclaimed one loudly. "Some real lookers. Let's go say hello."

Despite their intoxication, the men had little trouble negotiating the swaying aisle of the train.

Both came up to the women, each man wavering to the motion of the train and the influence of alcohol. The odor of their occupation followed the two cowboys. They smelled of horse sweat and manure.

"Say," said one of the men. "You girls wouldn't want a little company?"

"I should say not," replied Elizabeth. "Suppose you two go back to your seats."

"Lady," replied the one called Frank. "That ain't friendly. How about a little drink?"

Frank pulled a pint-sized bottle of whiskey from a vest and was about to offer it when George Temple appeared in the aisle and near the two drunks.

"Suppose I help you gentlemen back to your seats?" asked the bodyguard.

"Say mister, who are you to butt…"

George held something in his hand and it came down first on Frank's head and then on the other cowboy's hat and head. It made a thunking sound much like hitting a ripened watermelon. Both drunks began to fall. Frank collapsed back in George Temple's arms, and very swiftly, the bodyguard stepped over the other fallen man, half carrying and half dragging Frank up the aisle and to an empty bench. He sat the limp body down on it. Going back, he picked up the other man under the arms and easily moved him to the same bench. Both men's hats had fallen in the altercation, and George picked them up and returned to the unconscious fellows. He placed each hat in the manner of sleeping men. When he finished, many of the passengers began to applaud. George looked around and to Elizabeth's surprise, the bodyguard actually nodded his head at the other travelers and smiled. Returning down the aisle, he passed the conductor who had just entered the car.

"What's going on here?" demanded the train employee, directing his question at George. "I was told there was an altercation."

"Not too loud," replied the bodyguard. "Those two men up there are trying to catch some sleep."

Several passengers, hearing the reply, laughed. The conductor looked curiously at the two cowboys resting in their seats, shrugged his shoulders, and continued up the train car. Passing the two women, George looked down and winked. Elizabeth managed to whisper a reply.

"Was that necessary?" asked Elizabeth.

George stopped to answer.

"I know my business, and those two wouldn't have stopped. I've handled drunks for years now.

They'll sleep awhile, and when they wake up, they'll have headaches and won't feel like talking to anyone."

George continued to his seat. Then with a self-satisfied grin, he sat down and assumed his unobtrusive demeanor.

***

Elizabeth found that Blanche had fallen asleep. Behind her George Temple kept his vigil and remained virtually motionless. The man seemed to be unaware of anything, but Elizabeth knew that was a ruse. Uncle Henry would not hire an incompetent, and the last scene with the drunken cowboys was evidence of this. What an unusual experience her uncle had plunged her into.

Where would I be if it was not for Henry? she wondered. *I would still be moping around the house and reading through Father's papers. I would have become a hermit, perhaps even an old maid. There are so few men like father, or for that matter, like Uncle Henry.*

I will do what Uncle Henry wants; I will take an interest in the ranch. How grand it will be to ride a mustang and explore the land. I am so glad my father gave me a horse when I was little. I bet those cowboys will be surprised to see that I can ride.

They switched trains at Colorado Junction, six miles west of Cheyenne, and headed south on the Colorado Central for Denver. The long journey west was nearly over. Looking out the window, Elizabeth noted machine shops and factories, and then they passed over the Platte River. The train began to climb the rolling prairie and went by Argo and smelting plants. Eventually it descended into a valley and passed over Clear Creek Bridge. Excited now, Elizabeth woke Blanche, and together they stared out the window, noting high, flat-topped mountains. They entered a great chasm cut out of the rock. They rolled past more smelters, factories, and railroad machine shops to finally reach Golden, Colorado. Here they would meet a cowhand and ride by wagon to their ranch and their new home.

"Oh!" exclaimed Blanche. "It's all so exciting!"

This time Elizabeth had to agree.

At the depot, a group of immigrants crowded the platform. Those exiting the train added to the confusion. George Temple still hung back, holding on to his valise. Elizabeth and Blanche stood some distance away, holding their carpetbags. They deliberately packed light, knowing they would be purchasing Western clothing. When the crowd boarded and the platform cleared, all that remained were the three Easterners and a plump-looking man wearing Western clothes and sporting a wide sombrero.

"Would you be the Graham cousins?" asked the cowboy.

"We are," responded Elizabeth.

"Well, jumpin' Jehoshaphat!" declared the man. "You two are even purtier than the boss allowed. My name's Rusty, and I'm here to fetch you to the wagon."

After saying this, Rusty approached the young women, smiling ear to ear. He put out his rough mitt and, taking each of the girls' hands in turn, shook them up and down like working a pump handle. Hands thoroughly shaken, Rusty grabbed both carpetbags.

"Right this way," he called over his shoulder.

Elizabeth and Blanche followed; in the rear George Temple held back ten paces. With difficulty, they walked across the tracks. Before them stood a work wagon, and surrounding it was a group of five cowboys on their mustangs. When the men saw Rusty followed by the two women, they dismounted to meet their new bosses. Each man's face wore a huge smile.

"Whoopee!" yelled one of the cowboys.

This was followed by many exclamations of delight. One tall and deeply tanned ranch hand came forward, and his demeanor indicated that he was their leader.

"The Grahams?" asked the foreman.

"Yes," replied one of the cousins, stepping forward. "I'm Elizabeth and this is Blanche."

"Welcome to the Double TJ ranch. My name's Chapel Blue and I'm your foreman. The jaspers behind me are Lefty, Jake, Shorty, and Jack. You have already met Rusty."

"Chapel," said Elizabeth. "Such an unusual name!"

"I get that a lot," replied the man. "It was a name my Mother was fixed on. Most folks call me Chappy."

Saying this, he stepped forward and politely shook hands with each.

"Well...step up, boys, and meet our bosses. Show them that the Double TJ hands have manners."

Shyly, grinning and stumbling slightly, each of the other four men lined up.

“I’m Lefty,” said the first man, shaking hands with the girls.

“I’m Jake,” said the second.

“I’m Shorty,” said the third cowboy who was taller than even the foreman and stood a good six foot three.

“I’m Jack,” waved the last ranch hand. “Pleased to make your acquaintance.”

“I debated whether to let these hombres off to meet you ladies,” began Chappy Blue. “But it’s not every day we get new bosses, so we thought we’d do this up big and give you a guarded escort to the ranch. Are you ready to climb up on top?”

At this point, George Temple stepped forward. The bodyguard was wearing a bowler and an Eastern suit. His square-block frame stood out. He was an older man; it was impossible to determine his age. Despite his attire, he retained a powerful, muscular authority about him.

“Excuse me,” said Elizabeth. “This is George Temple. He’s an old family friend, and when we learned that we had been given the ranch, we asked him to accompany us.”

George stepped forward and reached out his hand to the ranch foreman. The two men seemed to measure each other with a handshake. George Temple stepped back first.

"I looked out for the ladies on the trip," said George. "Their uncle was a close friend of mine. As long as the ladies want me to, I'll continue."

"Of course, Mr. Temple."

"We appreciate the welcoming party, Mr. Blue," said Elizabeth.

"Please, call me Chappy," replied the foreman.

"Then I insist that you and the others call us Elizabeth and Blanche."

In answer, Chappy tipped his hat.

"Before we go to the ranch," began George Temple, "the three of us need to purchase clothing. We wish to visit the local mercantile. Perhaps you can advise us?"

"There's a general store up the street," replied Chappy. "I can give advice for you, but for the ladies, I'm afraid…"

"Shucks, boss," said Shorty. "There's the owner's wife who runs the ladies' section, and she'll be glad to help out Miss Elizabeth and Miss Blanche."

"Then let me help you aboard, and we'll be on our way," said Chappy.

The foreman stood by the front right wheel of the wagon and helped Elizabeth and Blanche climb up.

When Elizabeth sat down, she noted that their side of the wooden seat was covered in wool blankets.

"Thought a little padding might come in handy, Ma'am," said Rusty, smiling broadly.

"How kind of you," replied Elizabeth.

"What a large wagon," declared Blanche adjusting her position and looking around.

"It's the only working vehicle besides the chuck wagon," explained Rusty.

George threw up his carpetbag and went to the rear. He stepped on the hub of the wheel and climbed over. There were supplies for the ranch piled in the back. The bodyguard sat down on two-grain sacks and put a hand on the railing. Rusty slapped reins and two large horses jerked the wagon to a start. The five cowboys mounted and followed. Dust rose up in the street from the wagon wheels, and the ranch hands avoided it. It was a short jaunt up the street, and they halted before going to a general store.

The two women were greeted by the store owner's wife. They introduced themselves, began a conversation, and discovered that their presence had been anticipated. George Temple, being the man he was, went about selecting a Winchester 73 and purchased several boxes of .44-40's. With the jocular advice of the five ranch hands, he then selected clothing: a belt, a pair of boots, and a Western hat. When asked about a pistol, George pulled back his suit jacket and revealed double holsters with twin Colt .38s.

"Out here, a man wears a sidearm exposed," commented Chappy Blue. "You might want to consider doing the same. Besides, it's summer, and without a jacket, that rig would look a bit unusual."

"You made your point," replied George. "Let me have a left and right holster that'll fit these .38s and two pistol belts."

The women took considerably longer. When they finally came out of the store, the cowboys rushed to help carry and load the many bundles onto the back of the wagon. George lingered to pay the bill and then climbed aboard. Again, the ladies were helped onto the high seat, Rusty took up the reins, and the horses moved forward.

They followed a dusty road for miles, climbing over hills, zigzagging up steep inclines of small mountains and back down. It was a dry, arid country, and dust spewed from wagon wheels and horse hooves all the way to the ranch. Rusty finally drove the team under a wooden arch with the words Double TJ Ranch burned into the wood.

"What do the initials stand for?" asked Elizabeth.

"It's the past owner's brand, Miss Elizabeth," replied Rusty. "It stands for his name, Tommy Jackson. He was our boss and sold out to your uncle."

"I suppose it's as good a name for a ranch as any," said the young woman.

"Each cattle ranch has to have its own brand," explained the driver. "Folks here about know this brand, and it would be troublesome to change it now."

Flat land rose slightly with each forward movement up the road. The incline steepened, and in the distance, ranch buildings could be seen on a hill. A mountain loomed large behind the structures. On either side of the ranch, hills enclosed the land. Thousands of acres of grassland were contained on three sides by natural barriers. They protected the steers and horses.

When they reached the summit containing the buildings, the ladies both exclaimed surprise that the bunkhouse, attached cook shack, and home were constructed of adobe. There was a primitive beauty to the square construction and beige color. They blended in perfectly with the landscape. Only the distant barn, made of wood, stood out against the surroundings.

Climbing down from the wagon, Elizabeth and Blanche turned, and both gasped at the view. Looking back to the east, the high ground of the ranch revealed they had climbed thousands and thousands of feet above the open prairie. Before them loomed a hundred-mile view, clear to the purple horizon. They saw endless hills dotted with the green of pine trees, promontories, plateaus, and miles of yellow grassland. Turning to look in a full circle, they saw a chain of mountains to the south and west, some with snow on their jagged peaks. It would take hours to examine every feature, and still the eye and brain could not take it all in.

"Why it's just breathtaking," declared Blanche.

The cowboys, proud of the ranch and its amenities, beamed at the surprised rapture of the two women.

"Come," said Chappy. "I'll show the three of you the house, and then you can tell us where to put your things. Any change you want to get you settled, you just tell us, and we'll do our best to make it right."

There were three bedrooms to the adobe, and each had a door leading out onto a patio, one with a front view of the prairie and two with a back view of the mountains. Blanche and Elizabeth chose two identical rooms with views of the mountains, and George got the third opening in front. Each room had its own fireplace and the house was decorated with Western paintings, artifacts, and colorful Indian blankets. The floors were tiled and large wooden beams held up high ceilings. This was not the ramshackle home Uncle Henry had described but a substantial adobe ranch house built to last.

Chappy waited outside, and when the women came back, they were dressed in denim skirts and cotton blouses. On the porch they were met with a larger group of cowboys. Chappy introduced them with too many names to remember the first time around. To their surprise, Shorty, the tallest man on the ranch, was the cook. He announced that dinner would be served at five-thirty. The three were asked if they would take supper in the cook shack or in the house.

Elizabeth could tell that the question was important to the men, and they tried to appear nonchalant. The answer she gave would determine whether they would fraternize with the ranch hands or stay aloof and separate by having private meals.

"Shorty," replied Elizabeth to the tall man. "Blanche, George, and I will be having our meals in the cook shack. We wouldn't want you to have to perform any extra service."

Some of the men cheered, and the rest grinned.

"You hear that, boys?" called out Shorty, beaming ear to ear. "That means you fellers will watch your language around these two fine ladies and wash before comin' to the table."

"From now on it's a standing order," reiterated the foreman.

Some of the men groaned.

"Before supper," Elizabeth asked Chappy. "Could you show us where the ranch books are kept? I would like to start right in studying the finances."

"On the side of the house, there's a little office with an iron door," replied Chappy. "I got two keys. I'll hand them over. It's also where the safe is kept with a little cash money. Once a month, the men line up, and we make payroll."

Chappy led Elizabeth and Blanche to a side door facing the cook shack. A large, thick, Spanish-style door with iron bracing was opened with a skeleton key. Inside the room, a scarred desk and an office chair on rollers were found. Behind them was a heavy square safe. Against the wall was a floor-to-ceiling built-in bookshelf, upon which were piled dusty ledger books.

"It looks neat enough," said Blanche, peeking inside the room.

"I'm afraid Tommy Jackson was a terrible bookkeeper," said Chappy Blue. "There's all the books he kept since the ranch was started. But to tell you the truth, I couldn't make heads or tails of them. When he first purchased the ranch, your uncle left instructions. I was to keep up the record keeping. I'm no good at wrestling numbers, either. But I figured out my own system and it's those four small notebooks and the box sitting on the desk. The bank book I keep in the safe."

Elizabeth pulled back the rolling chair and sat down. She picked up one of the notebooks, and the first page was labeled *Income.* Below it were two entries from cattle sales, dated spring and fall. Picking up a second notebook, Elizabeth opened it, and on the first page was printed *Expenses.* Here were printed columns and columns of debt. Each entry describing the item purchased, the name of the business, and the amount. The majority of debt was to the general store. The third ledger contained a count of the livestock; only a few entries contained tallies of cattle, horses, and other farm animals.

"Where do you keep the receipts?" asked Elizabeth.

"In that cheese box," replied Chappy.

Elizabeth looked up and saw that the foreman's face was turning dark red. With difficulty, she tried to open the lid. The foreman had to hold down the bottom, and then the lid came off. Stuffed inside were piles of receipts.

"My," said Elizabeth. "We'll have our hands full putting this in order."

"Sorry, Miss Elizabeth," said Chappy. "Since taking over the ranch, I've not missed recording one bill, but as you see I could think of no other way of keeping the receipts. That final ledger on the desk is the payroll. It has each man's name and how much he was paid every month." Elizabeth took it up, opened to a page, and glanced at it briefly.

"I think that with Blanche's assistance, I will be able to go over the books within the next few days. Will you be available if I need more help understanding them after supper?"

"Yes, Ma'am," replied Chappy. "Day or night, you just send one of the boys, and they'll find me. If no one's around, go to Shorty, and he'll locate me. The cook has his own room in the cook shack. As for our work schedule, every night after supper, if you don't mind, I'll go over the next day's assignments."

"Is that how you did it with Mr. Jackson?"

"Yes, Ma'am."

"Will we get to see some of the ranch tomorrow?"

"Sure thing! The boys were mighty taken with you and Miss Blanche. They've been arguing over which horse to select for the both of you. It depends on how well you can ride and how much of the ranch you will be able to see."

"I can ride a little bit," smiled Elizabeth. "We start tomorrow?"

"You just say the time, and I'll have horses saddled and ready. Will Mr. Temple be going with you?"

"Since he will be advising us, I think he'll be as eager as the two of us to see the land."

At that point, the clanging of ringing iron could be heard. Startled, Elizabeth turned her head toward the sound.

"That's dinner; Shorty sure can make that triangle ring."

Blanche and George Temple came out of the house and joined Elizabeth and the ranch foreman in the cook shack. Inside were several small tables and one large one. When they entered, the cowboys were sitting. With a growl from Shorty, the men stood up.

"Miss Elizabeth, would you please sit here?" said Shorty smiling, his tall frame lengthened by a short white hat. "Miss Blanche, will you sit here, and George, here."

Shorty held the chairs out for the two women and scooted them up to the table.

"You men can sit," commanded Shorty. "Rusty, help me serve the ladies."

The cowboy picked up a meat plate, and while he held it, Shorty placed three large steaks on the newcomers' plates. Rusty set the steak plate down and helped Shorty serve the rest of the meal.

"Simple fare," explained Shorty, "but the men like filling portions. The beets and carrots come from the garden I keep behind the cookhouse."

"Perhaps after dinner you can show Blanche and me your garden," said Elizabeth.

Acknowledging that this was a special occasion for the cook, she was doing her best to show deference.

"Why it would be my pleasure, Miss Elizabeth," beamed Shorty.

There was a brief moment of silence and then the hungry men, forgetting their manners, began to frantically reach for food and fill their plates. Shorty, ready for the occasion, began banging loudly on a pan he had ready with a large wooden spoon.

"Before you men eat," shouted Shorty. "There will be a brief prayer. Rusty, suppose you do the honors."

The noise of plates being filled by the cowhands gradually abated, and Rusty, who had prepared the prayer in advance with Shorty's coaching, came to his feet.

"Ahem," began Rusty. "We'll bow our heads, boys."

Jack failed to lower his head and Shorty, standing nearby, hurriedly thumped him on the head with a spoon. Both Elizabeth and Blanche witnessed this, quickly looked at each other, put their hands to their mouths to hide a smile, and closed their eyes.

"Lord, we thank you for this food and for the hands that prepared it. We are humbly thankful for your bounty. God bless this ranch and thank you for sending such good owners as Miss Blanche and Miss Elizabeth. May the good Lord look out over us and help us prosper. Amen."

"Amen," repeated Shorty loudly.

This was followed by a staccato of "Amen" from the long, large table. There was another short silence, and then, with startling ferocity, knives and forks clattered loudly on heavy stone plates as the men began cutting steak and stuffing food in their mouths. Shorty, standing near the large table and over the men like a commander in charge of his troops, once again began banging on a pot with his wooden spoon.

"This ain't no race!" shouted Shorty.

Surprise showed on the men's faces, and they momentarily paused in their eating, then sitting somewhat straighter, remembered their manners. Again, Blanche and Elizabeth exchanged smiles. It was evident that the cowboys had made an effort to groom themselves before dinner. Many were sporting their best shirts. Each man had combed his hair, and evidently, a bottle of pomade had been shared as the sweet smell of the tonic was in the air.

After supper, the men exchanged greetings with the two women. They lined up to place their empty dishes and utensils in the cook's bucket of soapy water. Then, the men disappeared.

Shorty came forward.

"If the two of you would like to see my garden, I'd be mighty pleased."

Chappy stood nearby, relieved that the men had conducted themselves with a modicum of decorum.

"I'll go to my room now," he said. "If you need to speak with me or go over tomorrow\s work schedule, send Shorty, and I'll come up to the house."

"Before you go," said Elizabeth. "I have a question."

"Yes?"

"I noticed the men ate very well tonight, in fact, an enormous amount of food. Is that normal?"

"If you're asking if the cook is being overly generous, the answer is no. You see, the one thing the men expect is good food. For a cowboy to be loyal and ride for the brand, the most important aspect of any ranch is the food it serves. Serve bad food; it won't be long, and a ranch hand will saddle up and ride away. No amount of coaxing or money can get a cowhand to stay if the chuck is bad. Shorty is one of the best cooks around. Every time he goes to town, ranchers offer him more money to quit and work for them. Out here, a ranch is judged by how they feed their crew, not how much they pay."

"Thank you, Chappy, for explaining that to me."

"Not at all," said the foreman, putting two fingers to his sombrero and walking away.

Shorty went up and down the rows of the small garden showing which plants he was growing.

"It's a small garden, but I try to give the men vegetables I can't buy. Besides, I like gardening."

"I do, too," said Blanche. "Do you mind if I help? Have you ever tried planting tomatoes?"

"I thought they were poison," replied Shorty.

"No, they're simply delicious," said Blanche. "Look, we could work up the ground over there and plant a long row. I brought some seeds with me from New York; I always wanted to have a chance to raise them."

Elizabeth wandered off into the growing coolness of the night. The sun hadn't set, but all its heat was lost when it disappeared on the other side of the Western mountains. The constant contact with so many employees, all men, was going to be taxing. Chappy Blue was a mystery. He said little and seemed to stand by and observe everything. The books didn't really look like a difficult thing to go over. There was a spring and fall payment and the bills simply needed to be added up and deducted. It certainly looked like there were more bills than income. Somehow they must make the ranch a paying proposition.

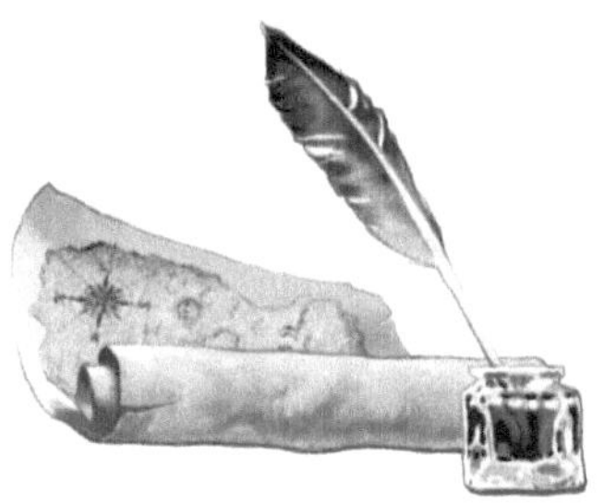

CHAPTER 10

The bell on the pawn shop door rang loudly as Leonard Newton entered. He was still dressed as a gentlemen, but wrapped in a cloth handkerchief was all that he owned of any value. A man wearing a green eyeshade and jeweler's glasses sat at the cage.

"May I help you," asked the proprietor.

"I have some jewelry I'd like to sell," replied Leonard.

"Place them on the counter, and I'll take a look."

Leonard took out the handkerchief and untied a loose knot. Gold and diamond rings were revealed. Four were men's rings, an impressive diamond necklace, and a woman's diamond ring Leonard had stolen from his mother's bedroom.

"Are they stolen?" asked the man in the green eyeshade.

"Of course not," declared Leonard Newton with heat in his voice. "These four rings are mine; these two pieces are my sick mother's. Very expensive pieces I might add."

"Maybe so," said the proprietor. "I'll give you a thousand for the lot."

"Why, that's robbery! They're worth three times that and more."

"Take or leave it," said the owner.

Leonard was impatient and wanted the money. Looking at the glass displays of jewelry, watches, and various other items of interest and seeing several pistols and rifles behind the counter, a sudden thought came to him.

"You're a thief, but I'll take the money."

Leonard's idea of robbing him solidified when the little man behind the counter opened a box stuffed with greenbacks. Leonard watched the proprietor take out a wad of paper currency and count a thousand dollars in bills.

"If you don't mind," said Leonard. "I'll take my money in coin. Where I'm going, they don't take folding money."

The shop owner replaced the cash and took up another box. This was stuffed with twenty dollar gold pieces. Leonard licked his lips as the money was counted out. In a calculated manner, he noted there were no windows and only one exit. A heavy iron door appeared to open to rooms in the back of the shop. No doubt the little man lived there.

Fifty twenty-dollar gold pieces weighed a great deal. The coins were evenly split into stacks of twenty-five and put in two cloth sacks with drawstrings. Leonard placed the two bags in each pocket of his suit coat. Turning abruptly, without saying another word, he left the pawn shop.

Leonard waited an hour, taking coffee and a sandwich in a restaurant up the street. From a window, he watched the pawn shop. There was an alley on one side and the room in the back must have a door that opened into the alley. Walking past the shop again, he looked into the narrow corridor. It ran between buildings until it met on another street. Right above and across from the alley was a run-down hotel. Leonard went in and registered under an assumed name. He asked for a room facing the street and was given one on the third floor.

Then, he went out and found a business that sold money belts. Purchasing wine, cheese, and bread, he returned to the hotel. Leonard sat near his room window, eating and drinking, watching the alley and pawn shop. Methodically, he placed the gold coins in the pouches of the money belt. Staying up all night, he saw little movement. It was early morning, just before dawn, when the old man from the pawn shop opened his steel door onto the alley and disappeared up the street.

Leonard Newton checked the charges in his pistol. It was a cap and ball Army Colt .44. He placed it in a left-sided shoulder holster. Taking up a dagger, the man slid it into a sheath on the right side of the holster. Putting on his suit jacket, he went to a cloudy mirror and looked at himself. There was no sign of the pistol, knife, or the money belt. Entering the hallway, he closed the door quietly and took the stairs. Outside, the sun was beginning to rise, and faint light illuminated the paved walk and entrance into the narrow alley.

Leonard walked towards the steel door where the old man had exited. Beyond it was an indentation in the bricks wide enough for a person to hide. He wedged his body into the space and waited. It wasn't long and the pawn shop owner appeared and turned into the alley. He was carrying a cloth sack of groceries in one hand, and in the other, he held a large skeleton key. Leonard waited until the little man turned the key and opened the steel door. Then the thief rushed forward, pushed the owner inside, and closed the door. The shop owner turned and, in the gas light of the back room, saw his assailant.

"You!" exclaimed the man. "I thought there was something suspicious…"

At the same time, the shopkeeper dropped his groceries and reached inside his jacket. In his right hand, he produced a single-shot derringer, which he instantly fired. There was a loud pop and Leonard Newton felt the impact of the .41 caliber bullet. It struck the thief in the belly and doubled him over in pain, the impact pushing air from his lungs. But the pain dissipated, and looking down, he saw that gold coins had stopped the bullet. Drawing his dagger from its sheath, Leonard plunged the knife into the shop owner's heart. The little man gasped and fell heavily to the floor. Leonard knelt down, and wiped the blood off the blade on the owner's clothing. Blood began to form a pool on the floor. In the flickering gaslight, the attacker smiled as he watched the shopkeeper struggle and die.

Leonard acted quickly, not knowing if anyone else lived in the back rooms. He opened the steel door and took the key from the outside lock. Then he closed it and made his way to the next room. It was a tiny kitchen. One doorway led to a small bedroom, and there appeared to be no one in it. Leonard returned to the pawn shop.

His heart pounding excitedly, he looked around and found a carpetbag. The two boxes of money he saw the day before were gone. Looking around, he discovered a floor safe, and it was locked. He had no way of opening it. Leonard cursed profusely, using every dirty swear word he knew. There were many drawers at waist level on the counter opposite the front door, and below them were the wooden backs of the glass display cases. The young man tried to open one, but it was locked. He was hesitant to break the glass and risk cutting his hands and wrists.

Anger and a cold ruthlessness took over the thief. Wishing he could punch and kill the little man all over again, he looked for a tool to break open the locked counter doors. A carpenter's box was sitting on the floor next to several rifles. Leonard took up a heavy screwdriver. Jamming the flat end into a drawer, he levered it back; the metal tore wood, and the drawer slid open. Leonard took several heavy gold watches with gold chains and placed them into the carpetbag. Opening several other doors he found some silver coins. Jamming open the last drawer, there were several black cases. In one, he discovered rings; another case contained gold and silver necklaces, and a third held loose diamonds and precious cut stones of various sizes and colors. These were of great value and somehow escaped being locked in the safe.

His heart was still racing from growing excitement, and he feared that too much time had passed. Leonard quickly forced open another display case and reached inside. He scooped up more rings, necklaces, and gold watches as quickly as he could. These he jammed into the carpetbag. In the last display case, he grabbed a double-barrel derringer and a converted Colt .38. These were put in his right jacket pocket. Then, a loud bang from the alley came to the young man's ears, and he gasped with excitement and fear.

Taking up the heavy carpetbag with its stolen contents, Leonard made his way to the shop's front door. There was a tiny window in the door and the young man looked out. It was broad daylight now and crowded with people. Gasping for air, Leonard turned and ran to the rear shop door. Opening it slowly, he peered outside. There was a man in the alley dumping refuse into a container. Leonard closed the door and waited. When he heard nothing further, he stepped outside. Taking up the skeleton key, he began to lock the door.

"Who are you, mister? Where's Henry?"

Leonard Newton turned around and saw a stocky man with an empty wooden crate in his hand. He was the one throwing refuse into wooden barrels. The thief, heart pounding, held tightly to the carpetbag. He let go of the key, turned, and ran.

"You! Thief! Help police! Help!"

Leonard ran up the alley as the next door shop owner continued to yell. The man threw down his wooden crate and attempted to run. He tripped on his club foot. Seeing part of a broken brick, the shopkeeper picked it up and threw it at the fleeing crook. It struck near Leonard, broke apart, and rolled. He ducked down and ran faster.

Coming out onto the next street, Leonard ran across it, up the walk, and disappeared into another alley. Police whistles began sounding. Fear gave the thief energy and speed, and he held tightly to the handles of the heavy carpetbag with his left hand. As Leonard approached another street a policeman appeared. Without slowing or thinking, Leonard pulled the pistol from his jacket pocket. Then he ran bodily into the uniformed officer and struck him heavily on the head. The policeman fell, and Leonard continued on.

After running through several alleys, gasping for breath, and sweating profusely, Leonard came out onto another street and stopped. He returned the pistol to his jacket pocket and walked along as normally as he could. Taking a handkerchief, he wiped the sweat from his forehead. More people were on the walkways. Leonard did his best to try to blend in. Horses and carriages moved up and down the street. He crossed at a corner and hurriedly stepped towards the train station carrying the heavy carpetbag.

Reaching the station, Leonard went inside and bought a ticket all the way through to Denver. Dressed in his elegant suit, he went into the train station restaurant and sat down. Through large windows, he watched uniformed policemen search the street and the crowd. Leonard ordered coffee and breakfast. The coffee came first, and he sat and sipped the hot black brew. Waiting for the train, the man's heart calmed to a normal beat, and slowly, he regained his confidence and began to believe he had gotten away with the robbery and murder. Leonard began to glory in the rush of excitement. It was better than anything he had ever felt in his life. He had at least five thousand dollars worth of jewelry and watches at his feet. Pawned slowly, he had more than enough to live on for several years.

When the time came, Leonard Newton picked up the carpetbag and walked toward the train. When he climbed aboard, the conductor offered to take his bag. Leonard declined, sat down, and set the bag at his feet.

CHAPTER 11

After leaving Shorty and his garden, Blanche met Elizabeth. Together, they took a path behind the house and went for a walk. With the sun setting behind the mountains, the day's heat was gone, and the late evening air began to cool to a comfortable temperature. Behind the two women, George Temple appeared, less than a hundred yards away. Looking back, they could easily discern that the bodyguard was carrying a rifle. Uncle Henry's friend was always vigilant and silent on the job.

"I've written a letter to Larry Roth," said Blanche. "If you could, I would like you to look at it. I think it's pretty good, but I want your opinion."

"Don't you think you should wait at least a week?" asked Elizabeth. "Not appear so eager?"

"But I am eager. He promised to come in a month, and I don't want him to lose interest."

"I hardly think he will, Blanche. But I'll be glad to look at your letter."

"Do you think he can really help improve this ranch? Tomorrow, we're going to be given horses and take a ride across it. Isn't it all so exciting?"

"Yes, it is," replied Elizabeth. "Suppose we head back before George has a fit. I have the key to the office. Maybe you and I can add up those columns of expenses and find out how much money is owed."

"Oh," said Blanche. "Do you think the ranch is in debt?"

"I'm afraid so. There seem to be a lot of bills. But without a mortgage to pay, perhaps we'll break even."

The women turned and started back along the narrow dirt trail that appeared to lead up into the mountains. George stood still and watched them return. From behind them, clear and far away, a wolf called. It was a lonely wail that echoed across long distances. The women stopped and listened.

"Oh, wasn't that so, so…" began Blanche.

"Yes, dear," said Elizabeth, "this a beautiful and mysterious place. Even the air is different."

Both smiled and breathed in the fresh Western aromas. The pungent odor of pinion, cedar, and ponderosa pine trees filled their lungs. Heat absorbed by the hard ground was now being released into the cooling air and against their bodies. The sensation was invigorating. Even though the sun had set, the dome of the sky was still an endless expanse of darkening blue. The extended views of the land were breathtaking.

The girls continued to walk, and when they came upon George Temple, his expression was a deep frown.

"Must you chase off somewhere without telling me?" asked George. "Don't you know that was a wolf? There are packs of coyotes, hydrophobia skunks, who knows what characters roam these mountains…"

"Wasn't the wolf's call wonderful?" asked Blanche.

"Chilling is the word I would use," replied George.

Behind them, in the distance, coyotes began to yip and make high-pitched calls. Another pack responded from a spot below them and began its incessant howling. A shadow passed over their heads and all three looked up to see a large owl. They watched it glide down the incline of the ranch, not once flapping its huge wings, sinking towards the ground to disappear.

"George," said Elizabeth, talking above the howling coyotes, "Blanche and I are going to the office to look at the books. You can join us, if you want."

"No, but it is very pleasant. I will take a chair and sit outside. I wonder what the rule is about getting coffee this time of the night."

"Why don't you go ask Shorty?" suggested Elizabeth. "I'm told he has a room behind the kitchen. Take your time, and before you come back, ask him to fetch Chappy in an hour or so. I need to talk to him about work plans for tomorrow."

"You two won't go running off…," began George.

"No," said Elizabeth. "We're both carrying the derringers, and I hardly think we'll run into any trouble sitting in the office."

Blanche and Elizabeth watched George set down the rifle near the office door and saunter off to the cook shack.

"When Larry Roth visits," said Blanche. "I hope George doesn't…"

Elizabeth laughed.

"The bodyguard is a sort of a pest, isn't he? Still, I must say he is dedicated; Uncle Henry would be proud."

Elizabeth used the large skeleton key on the lock and the heavy door opened with the turn of the latch. Going to the desk, she sat down. Blanche found a stool and sat at one end. Opening the large desk, Elizabeth searched for paper and pencils and found them. They worked at adding up deficit bills for an hour and George sat outside with a coffee cup in his hand. The foreman, being told there was no hurry, finally arrived and knocked on the door casing.

"You called for me?" he asked.

"Yes, Chappy," said Elizabeth. "I wondered if you and I could have a private talk."

"In the office?"

"If you don't mind, Blanche?"

"No, it's been a long day," said the pretend cousin. "I don't know about anyone else, but I'm going to bed."

"Just make sure she stays safe," said George to Chappy, and then the bodyguard followed Blanche into the house.

"I'll do that," responded the foreman.

"I changed my mind," said Elizabeth, using the key to lock the office door. "Shall we walk?"

"It's another nice night," said Chappy. "You lead the way."

The dark blue sky was slowly turning dusky black. Stars began to appear and pulse in the night sky. Coyotes far away kept up high-pitched howling. Somewhere an owl hooted and crickets made a rhythmic chirping. From time to time, a breeze whipped up and could be felt pleasantly wafting across their faces. The smell of the pine trees was pleasant.

They walked along in silence for some time, each apparently declining to begin a conversation.

"Are you always so…reticent?" asked Elizabeth.

"Ma'am?"

"So…quiet?"

"I've been accused of that. I suppose…it's best to observe…learn the lay of the land, so to speak."

"I see now why you were chosen to become foreman."

"Ma'am?"

"Have it your way, Chappy. But if we're going to work together you are going to have to be more candid with me. Tell me something about yourself; that may help."

"What do you want to know?"

"How you came to this ranch. Something about yourself when you were young, your schooling, places you worked. Things like that."

Chappy stopped on the trail and glanced briefly at Elizabeth, then at the ground. Then, abruptly, he looked up and studied the stars. She noted that he was tall and that his profile was very handsome.

"I'm not one to talk about myself," he began. "Leading these men, it's best not to reveal too much."

"Say something, Chappy," said Elizabeth. "After all, you're my foreman, and I have to learn to trust you and your judgment."

"What I tell you stays between the two of us?"

"Since I'll be more in charge of this ranch than Blanche, I want to know. I won't repeat what you tell me to anyone—unless there's a reason."

"There's nothing bad in my past. I just want you to know that. To maintain discipline, the less these men know about me, the better it is."

"Sounds lonely…"

"No, it's not. You have a fine outfit here. They're a swell bunch to boss."

"Then tell me who you are, Chappy, so I can know you better. And I promise what you say, I'll keep to myself."

Again, the foreman stared up at the sky. It was some time before he began to speak. Elizabeth thought that she had never met a more disciplined or quiet man.

"When I was a kid, my folks came west. Ma took ill and Pa quit the wagon train before we started. We settled in St. Louis. Ma died, and there was a younger sister and brother. Pa got work and I finished some schooling and started driving freight wagons around town. Eventually, I argued with my father, and I left. The railroad and steamships took up most of the freighting business anyway, so I got a job as a cowhand in Kansas. I was young and I learned. Later, I drifted to Denver and somehow ended up working as a deputy sheriff. After a while, I found out that being on a ranch was better for me. I knew Tommy Jackson from being a lawman. I asked, and he hired me as foreman."

"I see," said Elizabeth. "Could I ask you to tell me what you think of us coming to the ranch?"

"Ma'am? It's too early to…"

"Chappy," interrupted Elizabeth. "I want to know exactly what you and the men were discussing before we got here."

There was a long silence between them. More stars were coming out in the night sky and the moon was rising. Now the ambient light was bright enough to leave a shadow of the two persons standing on the prairie trail.

"You're asking me to tell on my men?"

"No, as your employer, I am asking you what concerns you and the men had about us before we arrived."

"The hands...the boys...had a running bet that you two were going to be as…"

"Yes?"

"As ugly as two horny toads."

"Well?" said Elizabeth, smiling despite herself. "Can you explain exactly how something like that came about?"

"If I remember right, Shorty kept saying that two beautiful New York doves were coming west and that the ranch would have the purtiest two bosses in the country. He kept saying that to the men over dinner, and they kept teasing him how they would be as—excuse the phrase—ugly as two fence posts. Pretty soon, it got all worked up into bets. I hear Shorty and Rusty heaped in a pile of cash over the affair."

"And, which way did you bet?"

"Ma'am, I'm the foreman. I didn't."

"Chappy, isn't it time you started calling me Elizabeth?"

"I reckon."

"As amusing as your betting story is, you and the men certainly had other concerns."

"Yes, we did. The general discussion was fear that you two women would learn the ranch wasn't a paying proposition, sell off the cattle, put the place up for sale, and turn us all out on our ears."

"No, Chappy. Blanche and I have no intention of doing that. Before we got here, we were told the place wasn't doing well. Blanche and I went over the bills and subtracted this fall's earnings. It looks like you're already several hundred dollars in deficit."

"In the spring, we'll sell off the cows that don't produce a calf—and a few horses," said Chappy. "That should pay most of the debt until the fall round-up."

"Still," said Elizabeth, "I wanted to ask you what it would take to make a bigger profit."

"Same as any ranch in the West," replied the foreman. "Water."

"You want to elaborate?"

"Oh," said Chappy. "The idea of it is fairly simple. With more water for irrigation, you have more grass. With more grass, you can support more cattle. The more calves, the more steers, the bigger the profit."

"What would it take to have more water?"

"Several dams, some large catch ponds, and ditches and pipes to move water and irrigate the land. It would take an engineer, and cost a lot of money. In heavy rain, you would want a way to release water. A poorly constructed dam, one that fails, would be a dangerous thing."

"What do you mean?"

"Erosion. Water would come pouring down, moving earth, trees, and rocks. It could strike and destroy poorly built dams, release even more water, remove the grass, dig up the soil, and ruin the ranch. Not to mention killing the animals, the men, and wiping out the buildings."

"I see. If we had more water, could we raise horses for sale? Maybe have more farm animals, do a little farming?"

"Horses, yes—other animals, farming?"

"Seeing how the men eat," said Elizabeth. "A lot of the bills at the general store are over food items. Couldn't we raise pigs, chickens, potatoes, and corn that would help feed the men? For that matter, raise grain for the animals?"

"With enough water, anything is possible, but I don't think the boys would take to farming or even know how to work the soil. And no respecting cowboy would raise hogs. In fact, getting a cowboy off his horse is a tough thing to do."

"Then we could hire someone to raise hogs and do the farming?"

"I suppose. Some of the homesteaders do that. They raise hogs and a few cattle. But for the big spreads, it would be something new."

"Don't you think it would help keep down the costs?"

"It could."

"Is there something more I should know about the ranch and the reason it's doing so poorly?"

"Yes. George Temple has been keeping an eye on you two, and it's a good idea. For the last few years, we've had cattle rustled. Not just an occasional steer, but whole bunches of them."

"Did you report it to the sheriff?"

"We did…eventually. But Ma'am, I mean…Miss Elizabeth, the law is mighty thin out here, not like New York City. Ranchers don't run to the sheriff for help; they do their own policing, so to speak. To put it bluntly, they find the rustler or horse thief and string em up to the nearest tree."

"You're joking."

"No, I'm not."

"Have you...has this ranch committed such an act?"

"We have, twice. But most were shot and killed in a running fight, before we caught a live one."

"You've hung a man just for…"

"If we hadn't hung the rustlers we caught, they would have gone to jail, and eventually, there might have been a trial, and they may or may not have been sent to prison. But the word would have gone out that the Double TJ Ranch was soft, and pretty soon, every rustler in the county would have descended on the place, and there wouldn't have been a steer or horse left. Besides, the laws are different out here; the sheriff expects a rancher to take care of the problem himself, not waste the county's time with unnecessary jail and trial fees."

"That's the truth? You're not somehow…"

"It's God's honest truth, Ma'am. You can't mollycoddle a rustler and expect to have any stock. It's the way it is out here. Fact is, if you decide to, there won't be a horse, a cow, or, for that matter, a cowboy left on the place for you to boss. These are proud men who ride for the brand. They take their job of watching the herd mighty serious."

Elizabeth was agitated now and began to walk faster. They moved together under the moonlight, not saying a word. Feet crunched over hard, flinty ground, and the insects continued to chirp.

"I see being a rancher is harder than what I thought. I'll have to think about what you said. Now tell me the truth Chappy, what else do I need to know?"

"Well...you being a greenhorn, you can't expect to learn it all in one day. But there is one more thing you and Blanche need to know."

"What's that?"

"May I speak plain, Miss Elizabeth?"

"Please do."

"How do I put this?" Chappy questioned out loud. "You two need to be warned. Women, especially two pretty women such as yourselves, are a rare thing out here. Once the men in town and cowboys on other ranches get sight of the two of you, all heck will break loose."

"Whatever are you talking about?" asked Elizabeth, stopping on the trail and staring up at her foreman.

"This. Once you're seen…in town, at church, wherever you go, and word gets out, every single cowboy from eighteen to fifty will come calling. And, if you go to one of the Saturday night dances, you and Miss Blanche will be mobbed. Cowboys will line up two deep for a chance to dance with you. I warn you, they'll dance your legs off, and won't take no for an answer. As far as that goes, I expect cowboys, once they get sight of you, will quit their jobs or come on weekends and come flockin' out here to the ranch."

"You can't be serious."

"I am. Once the words out, men from fifty miles away will be all fired up to come courtin', and it'll be you that will have to handle the lot."

"Chappy Blue, you can't expect me to take this seriously. I think you're humoring me and I refuse to accept what you're saying."

"Have it your way, Miss Elizabeth, but you'll find out for yourself. You asked me to tell you what you needed to know, and this here, what I just told you, is for certain true."

"Suppose we head back now," said Elizabeth. "I don't have a jacket, and there's a chill in the air."

They walked back to the house without further conversation. At the adobe, Elizabeth stopped to share her final thoughts.

"You have told me a lot about the ranch. Things I needed to know, and I appreciate it. As for this warning about the cowboys, that I refuse to take seriously. In any case, we will have to find a way to make this spread pay. You should know that a man, Larry Roth, a rancher friend of Blanche's is coming to visit. This is something she arranged. You are my foreman and I don't want to insult you, but he will be here in a few weeks to look over the ranch and give advice. I want you to meet him, extend all courtesy, and just consider the suggestions he makes."

"I will do as you say," replied Chappy.

"Good, then we will see you tomorrow morning, and you can show us more of the ranch."

"Breakfast is at six, Miss Elizabeth," said Chappy. "After that, we'll show you the horses we've picked out for the three of you to ride."

"Good night then," said Elizabeth as she turned to open the door and disappear into the ranch house.

CHAPTER 12

Leonard Newton departed the train in Denver, went to a store, purchased Western clothing of his taste, changed into them, and discarded his fancy suit. He filled a sack with food items at a general store and paid for them. Entering a gun shop, he purchased cartridges for the pilfered derringer and the converted Colt .38. Then he selected a fancy engraved belt and holster with bullet loops and decorated with silver conchos.

Locating a land agent, Leonard examined a map on the wall.

"That's the property I want," he said, pointing. The description was of a small cabin with several acres of land, located some distance from town. "How much?"

"Already spoken for," said the agent.

"Yeah, by me," snarled Leonard, slamming down a bag containing twenty-five gold pieces.

The land agent counted out the coins.

"I promised it to another feller for the same amount, but he didn't put any money down."

Leonard gave the man one more gold coin and said, "A bird in the hand is worth two in the bush. Now fill out that title."

The land agent hesitated and looked up at the buyer. The man was intense, and his behavior was chilling. Reluctantly, the agent took the money and filled out the deed.

At a livery, he picked out a spirited mustang and purchased a used saddle and tack. Following directions, he rode to his newly acquired cabin and found it crude but adequate for his needs. Removing loose floorboards, he dug a hole with a rusty shovel, wrapped the carpetbag in an old canvas, and carefully buried the stolen treasure. Sitting at a roughly made table, the former New Yorker, burned wood in a rusty stove. He heated the cabin, prepared himself a meal of warm beans, bread, and cheese, and contemplated his next move.

CHAPTER 13

"For the ladies," said Rusty. "We picked out these two gentle mares. There's a bay and the gray. The white gelding is for George. We figured he could handle a spirited horse. Once you select your mount, usually it's yours for as long as you stay on the ranch."

"I've done a lot of things in my life, but one thing I know for certain in my past is that horses and I don't get along," said George Temple. "I'd much rather pick one of the mares."

A group of cowboys gathered around the corral. They stood as if bored; most were smoking or leaning against the railing. Two cowhands held the white, bridled, saddled, and blindfolded. The mount was tense and shaking. It was obvious that this was no ordinary horse. The men had come for a show, and it looked like George was backing out.

"Come on, George!" yelled Jack. "Ride the bronc!"

Elizabeth was dressed in men's canvas pants. She had on cowboy boots with the pant legs tucked into the tops. She also wore a shirt, a cotton jacket, and a Western sombrero on her head. Her hands sported tight-fitting leather gloves. Blanche was standing by and similarly dressed.

"I'll give the horse a try," said Elizabeth.

"Ma'am," replied Rusty. "This horse is…"

"You saddled him," said Elizabeth, "I'll ride him."

With that statement, she quickly climbed over the corral fence, jumped down, and walked toward the blindfolded mustang. There were two cowboys controlling the white, one holding reins and the other the horse's bridle.

"Miss Elizabeth," said one of the hands. "We was just funnin' George. This here cayuse can't be rode."

"I'd like to try," the woman replied.

"Chappy!" yelled Shorty. "Don't let the boss lady git killed!"

The foreman vaulted the fence and came up to Elizabeth, who was attempting to get on the left side of the horse. The gelding smelled her, snorted, shook its head violently, and began to fight the reins.

"The boys were just having a little fun with your man," said Chappy. "If you want a more spirited mount, we can find one for you, but not this one. This horse can't be ridden."

"If the joke was good enough for George, then it's good enough for me," replied Elizabeth.

"We don't want you to be hurt," said Rusty.

Other cowboys made comments of agreement.

"If you were willing to let George take a tumble, why not me?"

"Because you're a woman," blurted out one of the men.

"Out here, we protect women," said Chappy. "The boys wanted to test George's metal, not yours."

Ignoring the men before they could react, Lizzy put her left foot in the stirrup and hands on the pommel. Agilely, she swung her body up and a leg over the saddle to take a seat. She slipped her boots into stirrups up to her heels.

"Give me the reins!" commanded the lady.

The mustang screamed and bucked. Two men handed the reins to the rider. Then the cowboys, holding the horse's bridle, stepped back. Once Elizabeth had hold of the reins, Chappy himself jerked the blindfold free from the halter. No longer blind, the white exploded into movement, bucking, jumping high, and fishtailing back and forth. The cowboys, getting a show they never expected, began to shout and cheer their lady boss on. To their surprise, the young woman held her seat, holding two reins in one hand and a fist in the air as the horse hopped, bucked, and swirled around the corral. The mustang screamed its displeasure in piercing tones. Lizzy held her seat, using muscles from years of riding, and clamped her legs tightly to the horse's sides.

Enthralled, men tore sombrero's from their heads and waved them in the air. Many shouted out encouragement.

"Ride em, girl!"

The white bucked viciously and repeatedly rose higher in the air. Then, the mustang landed on all fours, jarring Elizabeth from her seat while at the same time making a twisting turn to the right. The young woman flew from the saddle and landed hard on her side. The horse's hooves pounded over her, and miraculously, she was not hurt. The horse screamed triumphantly and pounded across the corral, still bucking, empty stirrups flapping.

Chappy and two other cowboys came down from the corral railing and ran to their boss. Taking no chances, one of the men watched the mustang while Chappy bent over the prone woman.

"Are you hurt?" shouted the foreman, his concern clearly showing on his face. "I should have never let you take the chance."

The other men stood stone silent waiting breathlessly to see if Miss Elizabeth was hurt.

"Only my pride," replied the woman, coming to her feet.

The bystanders cheered, and a new respect among the hands went up for the boss lady.

The mustang was still bucking and twisting, but now it was circling and coming across the corral. The horse was furious and it lowered its head and bared teeth. Chappy and the other hand, none too gently, jerked Elizabeth back, and together they ran to the fence where they lifted her high off her feet. Men were already there to catch her as she was handed over the railing. The men jumped up and over just before the angry horse viciously snapped its teeth at empty air. Elizabeth, now safely on her feet and away from the furious mustang, laughed while she brushed the dirt from her clothes.

"You're right," she exclaimed. "That horse can't be ridden."

The cowboys whooped. Chappy and two hands were back in the corral. They were busy roping the white and tripping the horse's legs up with a third lasso. Ropes were tied tightly, and they left the horse on its side, kicking and screaming out its anger.

"All right, boys," shouted Chappy. "You've had your fun, now back to work!"

"Our boss lady sure can ride!" shouted Shorty.

The men hoo-rawed.

"Rusty and Jack," said Chappy. "You two were behind this so you grab the tack off that white and see to it that hoss gets to the back corral. We'll sell it first chance we get."

"Wouldn't give a nickel for that hombre," said Jack.

"All right, men, bring Miss Elizabeth that black," ordered Chappy Blue. "We've got a ranch to show."

Two hands brought a spirited horse intended for George. Since Elizabeth showed she could ride, she was given the mount.

Chapter 13

"Oh," said Lizzy. "He's beautiful. What's his name?"

"Yours to choose," said Chappy.

George got on the bay and Blanche, who had never ridden a horse, got on the gray. The two Easterners looked nervous. They sat awkwardly, legs splayed uncomfortably around the horse's bellies.

They spent the morning riding down through the grasslands to the northeast corner of the ranch. Jack and Rusty accompanied the group. The yellow grass from high up looked almost flat. But, they soon discovered the land undulated up and down. Occasionally, they had to cross deep arroyos that descended down steep inclines. It took time to find a way out and this was by foot, pulling on horse's reins to ascend the banks. At places there was rocky ground and very little grass. In other prairie meadows, the grass grew in profusion from the spring and summer rains and stood nearly three feet tall.

George and Blanche were sore and saddle weary by noon despite frequent stops to rest chafing skin.

"This is awful," said Blanche. "I never dreamed riding was so painful.

"You'll get used to it," said Jack. "Honest you will. Then riding a cayuse like yours will be pure pleasure."

"Not today, it isn't," replied Blanche.

They had ridden miles across the ranch. They now sat on a thousand foot plateau, completely level and thick with grass. The views from the promontory revealed thousands of acres of rolling yellow grassland as far as the eye could see.

Jack and Rusty were prepared. They set about gathering stones for a fire pit and emptying saddlebags. Before long, there was steaming coffee, bacon, beans, and bread. Plates and cups were filled and rocks were found and rolled up for the girls to sit on.

"How much of the ranch have we seen?" asked Elizabeth.

"We've come about five miles and ridden across some of the lower part of the ranch," replied Chappy. "There's a lot of grass here, more than what I thought this time of the year. We'll run the herd over here soon to graze. Still, it's mighty dry, and water is the problem. Always is. In this desert land, we calculate it takes about forty acres to feed one steer. But if they have to travel far to find water, they're running the weight off em'."

"How much water does a cow have to have a day?" asked George.

"Depends on the weight of the animal and how hot or cold it is," replied Jack.

"Lot of discussion about that there," interjected Rusty. "A full grown cow or steer needs about twelve to eighteen gallons minimum."

"That's a lot of water," said Blanche.

"Water we don't have way down here," said Chappy. "If we got the grass, we don't have the water, and if we have the water, we don't have the grass."

"That's what dams and irrigation would solve?" asked Elizabeth.

"Yes," replied the foreman.

"Still," said Rusty. "The men have to guard the herd from coyotes, wolves, catamounts, and those durn rustlers. Until we get rid of the rustlers, the herd's never safe."

They ate their lunch, rested for half an hour, packed up, and swung up on their mounts. This time, they headed straight west, and each step of the horse was up a slight incline toward the mountains. By late afternoon, they had traveled many miles. Here, it was mostly rock. When they came to a wide canyon, they stopped and rested.

"I want to show you something, Miss Elizabeth," said Chappy.

"I can't walk or ride another step," said Blanche.

"I could if my life depended on it," said George. "But I won't if I don't have to."

"You two rest," said Elizabeth. "I'm not sore at all, and the Western saddle is sure more comfortable than riding English. Having that pommel to hold onto now and then is useful. Chappy, you just lead the way, and I'll follow."

"We don't have to ride," said the foreman. "I can show you the canyon on foot."

He walked some distance following a wash. It twisted and turned and was full of gravel and tightly packed sand. Eventually they walked between two walls of rock that rose up on both sides of the arroyo. Here the canyon was narrow. Then, it opened up into a hidden valley containing many acres. They entered the valley, and it was surrounded by solid rock rising hundreds of feet.

"Here would be one likely place for a dam," said Chappy. "As you see, it's a natural enclosure. It would hold back the winter melt off in the spring and any rains that might come anytime. The volume of water would be deep, but if the dam failed, it would be bad. That's why you need an engineer to construct it. Make sure it held and would be safe."

"Oh, it's so lovely in here," said Elizabeth.

"Yes, it is," replied the foreman. "It's a bad place to be during a storm. Each time it rains, a wall of water comes rushing down. Sometimes, it's inches; other times, depending on how hard it rains, it becomes a muddy flood of rolling rocks and trees. The engineer would sure have to know his business."

"I see now what you mean," said Elizabeth. "How many more canyons are like this one?"

"There's three more, and several washes, and likely places for smaller dams and catch ponds. Some could hold water the entire year. But this is the largest canyon. With the dam, the cattle could graze and never have to walk far for water. They'd fatten up and we could double the size of the herd."

"That would turn a profit for sure!" exclaimed Elizabeth.

They headed back. Climbing up an incline and to the mouth of the canyon, Elizabeth slipped on a smooth slab of rock and slid backward. Chappy was behind her and he caught her in his arms.

"Oh!" exclaimed Elizabeth.

Chappy held her close, her back against his chest and his large arms encircling her. She held her breath and did not move, and she was certain he held her a few seconds longer than necessary.

"I'm sorry, that was so clumsy of me."

"That's all right," said Chappy. "You weren't clumsy this morning when you rode the bronc."

"I did pretty good, didn't I?"

"You sure did. You've ridden all day without complaint, and your interest in the ranch…"

"Yes?"

"You're gonna be a boss to make us plumb proud."

They walked to the horses without further conversation. George and Blanche were resting and getting back on their mounts; they both complained. Hours later, just before dark, they reached the corrals and dismounted.

"I'm going to bed," said Blanche.

"Without supper?" asked Jack.

"I'm too tired to eat," said Blanche. "And I'm not getting back on a horse for a long time."

"You'll stiffen up," said Elizabeth. "You better try riding a little tomorrow, or you'll be sorry."

"But Lizzy," said Blanche. "I just couldn't."

"You want to meet Larry and tell him you can't ride a horse?"

"All right, maybe tomorrow, but just let me go to bed."

George and Elizabeth headed for the cook shack while the men attended to the horses and put away the tack.

"I'm so hungry," said George. "I could eat a whole horse. Preferably, the one that made me so darn sore."

"George!" said Elizabeth. "You can't mean that!"

"Oh, but I do," replied the strong-willed bodyguard limping toward the cook shack, "I most certainly do."

CHAPTER 14

Weeks went by and Leonard Newton began to adapt to his Western surroundings. He stopped shaving and let his mustache, beard, and hair grow. He rode to town at night and lingered over dinner and coffee. Leonard kept his ears open and his mouth shut and listened to the gossip of restaurant customers. Sauntering up and down the streets of town, he watched the people and how they behaved. At night he entered various saloons and spent time playing a little poker and drinking sparingly. Already, he heard a conversation about the two pretty women named Graham who had inherited a fifteen thousand acre ranch. That would certainly have to be Elizabeth and her traveling companion.

She was using an assumed name and it had to be for a reason. And, that reason would have to be about money. The young woman didn't want others to know she had it.

Leonard eventually found a bar of his liking, a place where the rougher elements of town came to drink and gamble. He began to frequent it every night and play poker. By staying sober, when he appeared to drink along with the other men, it was easy to begin to win. By listening and keeping his eyes and ears open, he learned these men were involved in less-than-honest work.

"Say, Lenny," said one of the poker players one night. "Who in the Hades are you?"

"The names not Lenny or Len," replied Leonard Newton. "It's Leonard."

"Oh yeah?" said the Westerner. "Well, I'll call you what I want. And besides…I'm tired of you winning all the time."

"If you don't like to lose, don't play."

"Why you smart-mouthed dude! I'll show you!" began the angry and drunken man and he reached for a pistol.

Leonard sat calmly, a derringer already in his hand, and cocked. When the revolver of the other man cleared leather, Leonard fired. The bullet slammed into the wrist of the angry poker player.

The pistol fell to the floor, and the man jumped to his feet, blood dripping from his right wrist. Five friends of the poker player surrounded him and they confronted the new man.

"Who are you, Mister?" asked the leader of the group. "You've been hanging around our place for two weeks now. Just suppose you tell us why."

"My name is Leonard Newton, and I'm looking for a few good men to do a job for me."

"Yeah? This ain't no workhouse."

"I believe it is…for the kind of job I have in mind."

"What makes you think we'd work for you?"

"Money, a plan, and a way to get more," responded Leonard.

He was still holding the derringer in his hand and exposing it so the man he was talking to could see it was a double barrel and pointing in his general direction.

The leader of the rough crowd licked his lips and stared at the stranger. Leonard looked back, dark eyes shining hard out of a black-bearded face. Slowly, the outlaw leader began a faint grin that widened into a smile and then a laugh.

"All righty Leonard, suppose we talk about it."

"Not here. Too many ears. I prefer we meet somewhere out of town."

"What makes you think you can trust us?" asked the leader.

"I got ears, I got eyes," said Leonard. "What I have in mind…I need men like you. Men who aren't afraid to act for money."

"Why should we trust you?"

"By what I got to say and what I'm willing to pay. Meet me tomorrow at noon behind Miller's Rock and we'll talk about it. Leave that fool with the hole in his wrist behind. I don't want him."

"This better be good, Mister," said the outlaw leader. "Or…"

Leonard threw down two twenty dollar gold pieces on the table.

"Buy your men some drinks, I'll see you tomorrow."

With that statement, Leonard Newton got up from the table, still holding the derringer. The man with the wounded wrist had sat back down and was trying to wrap a handkerchief around the bleeding wound. The leader and four men stood watching the newcomer leave.

"What do you make of that, Jacob?" asked one of the outlaws.

"He's a killer," said the leader, picking up the gold coins. "I could see that straight off. And...a man with a plan, whether we'll go for it, is another thing."

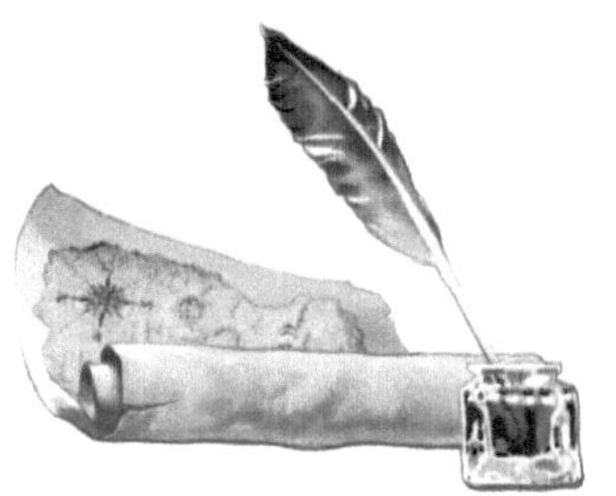

CHAPTER 15

Larry Roth read Blanche's letter over for the hundredth time and the paper was beginning to wrinkle and wilt from the frequent handling. The first part of the letter talked about the pleasure of meeting him on the train and how brave and strong he was in helping hand out food to those poor immigrant children. Blanche told him that he was welcome to come look over their ranch and make suggestions to improve it. She wrote in her letter that it would be good to see him again, and she hoped he would respond and tell her what day of the last week in October he would arrive. There was a post script. *I still have your golden coin and I hold and look at it every day.*

"You treasure and read that letter like your life depended upon it," said Benny Roth, Larry's father.

"That's because it does, Dad."

"Balderdash! You meet some Eastern girl on a train and you go lovesick on me. How could you get to know someone in a few minutes? I knew I should have used that belt on you more when you was a child. You're too headstrong; that's what it is. Meet some Eastern floozy and…"

"Careful, Dad!" declared Larry putting the letter down and rising to his feet. "Don't…"

Mister Roth was a foot shorter than his son and when the young man rose to his full height and began to advance in anger, the successful ranch owner unconsciously backed up.

"All right then! Go see that gal. But...if you stay too long, expect me to follow. Son, you don't know nothin' about women. Why does it have to be an Easterner? What's wrong with some hard-workin' Western gal who knows how to cook, and clean… knows her way about a ranch."

"'Cause all the ones I met act and look like men! You just wait, Dad, until you see her and meet her. Then you'll understand."

CHAPTER 16

Henry Burnett opened the letter from his niece with more energy than he had shown since she departed on the train with her traveling companion and the bodyguard. It was a long and thorough letter explaining their trip and arrival, with many details about the ranch, the men, and the land. Henry read it through hurriedly, then poured himself a cup of coffee, sat at the table, and read the letter again.

So she likes the ranch, thought Henry. *When she mentions the men, she talks about Shorty, the cook, and the cowboys. She describes the land in great detail, the wide open scenery, and the routine of the ranch work, and she writes paragraphs about riding her black mustang every day with the foreman to oversee the place. Interesting how she says so little about him. She says nothing about missing New York. Perhaps I have lost my niece to this ranch and to the West. The tone of the letter is so...so... enthusiastic. It is lonesome without having her here. Still, I am glad she has found a meaningful purpose in her life. I wonder...no...I hope I have done the right thing by my brother, in sending his daughter west.*

Now, if I could just get this factory to make a profit. I fired the former owner's staff. The men I brought in should turn it around. The workers were given a raise, and as the new owner, I told them the truth. It was up to them if they wanted to keep their jobs by turning a profit. Perhaps in six months we will see. I know the product is a good one. With Elizabeth gone, I have lost all patience. As soon as it turns, the very day, I'll buy a ticket west.

Henry got up, found paper and pencil, and began writing a response. Whatever money Elizabeth needed, whatever plans she came up with, he wrote, he would support her. Everything she said about water, grass, and raising more cattle seemed logical. Hiring an engineer to survey, design, and construct dams seemed reasonable.

The girl always did have a head on her shoulders. Maybe being in clean, fresh air and riding every day will help. After all, it was for her physical and mental health that I sent her out there. And, of course, to find a good man.

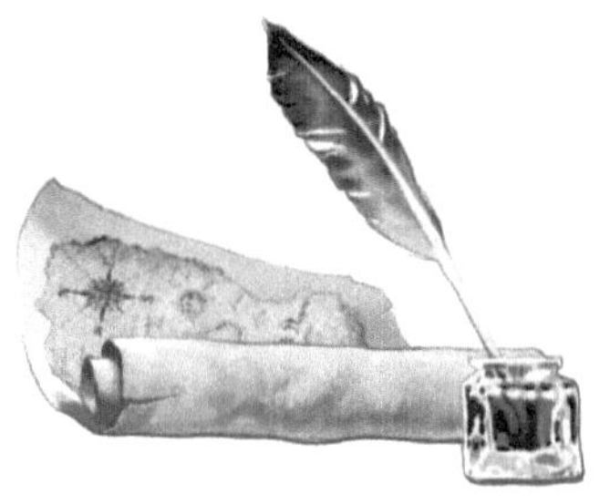

CHAPTER 17

Since the pretty new owners of the Double TJ Ranch arrived, three things had changed with the cowboys. They washed more often, combed their hair, and improved their language, at least while around the women. Perhaps a fourth thing had changed as well. The men were proud of their beautiful bosses and worked hard to please them. Their disposition was better, they smiled more often, and they NEVER missed a meal, for they knew for certain that the ladies would be at breakfast, lunch, and dinner. Ordinarily, Western men would resent the ownership and authority of women. But this was different. Didn't Miss Blanche and Miss Elizabeth refuse to sell out? Didn't they promise to keep the men working and try to improve the place? And didn't Elizabeth get up on that bucking bronc and show what stuff she was made of? The men pinched themselves every night, for what ranch in a thousand miles had such bosses as theirs?

Every cowboy on the place was in love with one of the two women. They mooned over them, brought them wildflowers, and spoke as graciously to them as their limited education allowed. It would have been amusing, but for all the bowing and scraping and sick calf looks the cowboys gave their bosses. What mitigated the circumstances to some extent, was that Elizabeth and Blanche recognized they must treat the hands with dignity and respect.

There wasn't any place on the ranch where the women could go without a cowboy fawning over them. It was, as Elizabeth described to Chappy Blue, a bit amusing but for its utter silliness. Only Chappy seemed to be immune to the ladies' charms, and he maintained a professional demeanor as a foreman at all times.

"That's Westerners for you," explained the foreman. "So far, there's twenty men to one woman out here. Some places, it's worse. And I don't think there are two women as attractive as you and Miss Blanche anywhere in the whole West. I told you it would be like this. Just wait until word gets out. If you go to the Saturday night dance as you plan this weekend, you'll find out for sure that every word I said was gospel truth."

And it was, men lined up two deep to dance, and while waiting, argued, pushed, and shoved each other to be next. Blanche, at first, was excited and all smiles that so many men vied to dance with her. Halfway through the night, her smile faded, her feet began to hurt, and she was too tired to go on. The many cowboys had to accept that Blanche needed to sit and rest.

Elizabeth was more practical about the avalanche of male advances. She danced to several different songs and then keeping Shorty the cook as her companion and guard, went outside to sip lemonade and sit down. Shorty was the tallest man around and Elizabeth used his height and strength to her advantage. He was all puffed up with pride, and all night long, he did not shirk his duty. Elizabeth survived the onslaught without becoming worn out by the countless suitors. Every man lined up to ask at least once for a dance and a chance to talk to the prettiest woman they had ever seen. It was Shorty's companionship that kept the men from sweeping Elizabeth away.

Glad to be back at the ranch, Blanche and Elizabeth went to bed at two in the morning. They both slept in and missed breakfast. Shorty, who had cooked up a big meal was still bursting with pride over being Miss Elizabeth's escort. He was hurt that the women didn't show up for breakfast, but then he understood they had come home late and were tired.

"Shorty, you didn't have to hog the boss lady all night long," complained Jack.

"Yeah!" protested many of the men over their chuck.

"Shut up and eat your breakfast!" shouted Shorty, holding command with his wooden spoon, frowning furiously but all the time smiling inwardly.

Blanche, Elizabeth, and George came to the noon meal and ate hungrily along with the cowboy crew.

"Miss Elizabeth," said Chappy. "Today's Sunday and the boys are laying off. Still, I want to see how the grass is doing to the west. Would you like to ride along?"

"Why, Chappy," replied Elizabeth. "Just because we went out last night doesn't mean I'll want to miss a good ride. Maybe we could push some of the cattle off the upper graze. It is getting pretty thin up there."

"That's why I want to take a look. Ever since this ranch began, all that good grass has gone to waste, except, of course, when it was cut. But hands hate that kind of work."

"Maybe in the future, we should purchase equipment and hire workers to put up hay," said the ranch owner.

Elizabeth liked saddling her black. She called the gelding Salty because that was the cowboys' expression for a tough hombre. Most often the mustang behaved itself, but from time to time, it would act up due to its high spirit. The horse could throw her if she didn't maintain a firm seat. Chappy wanted to get her a more reliable mount, but Elizabeth refused because she was becoming very fond of the black. A good rider, as long as she kept control, she would handle him.

The lady ranch owner demanded to follow what the cowboys did. But, she realized that learning to rope and perform more vigorous tasks was a bit beyond her ability. However, she did like catching and saddling her own horse.

Both Chappy and Elizabeth carried a rifle in a scabbard. There were elk, antelope, and mule deer on the range, and Elizabeth looked for the chance to shoot one and bring it to Shorty to cook. It was part of the bounty of the ranch, so why not take advantage?

The October afternoon was like nearly every day in Colorado, clear azure skies, only a few clouds off over the mountain peaks, and a bright shining sun that gave off heat. The temperature was above seventy degrees but riding under the sun felt warmer. They rode west along a trail the cowboys took daily to guard the herd. This being high desert country, dry and arid, once a trail formed in the hard adobe clay, it remained devoid of vegetation.

The cattle had eaten the grass close to the ground, and for miles and miles, it looked like a well-mowed park. They rode toward the mountains, and with each step of the horses' hooves, they went upwards. Puffs of dust rose up and fell. The riders sat back and enjoyed the scenery. Before them, the long row of mountain peaks ran north and south as far as the eye could see. Higher up, moisture came more often and lingered at the cool altitude. There the large Ponderosa pines grew.

Following the contours of the trail, the horses climbed down and up out of a deep wash. A steep hill was before them, and they followed the trail around it. When they came out onto open grassland, they spotted riders below them moving a herd of ten steers.

"I thought you said…" began Elizabeth.

"Rustlers!" whispered Chappy. "Get back to the wash before you're spotted! I'll handle this!"

"Not on your life!" hissed Elizabeth.

"Then quick!" ordered the foreman. "Ride back behind that hill before we are…"

Too late, the five rustlers spotted the two Double TJ riders. Several of the thieves pulled rifles and were already aiming and firing. Chappy spurred his horse and leaned far out, grabbing Elizabeth's black's reins. Bullets whizzed close as Chappy guided both horses and riders behind a hill.

"What are you doing?" asked an angry Elizabeth. "You're not going to let them get away with stealing my cattle!"

"You won't enjoy nothin' with a bullet in your brisket," declared the cowboy.

Chappy pulled reins and both horses skidded to a halt. Elizabeth's mount crashed into the rear of her foreman's horse. She grabbed the pommel to retain her seat, recovered, and reached for her Winchester. Jumping down, Elizabeth began to run straight up the hill. Seeing it was impossible to control his headstrong boss, Chappy followed her lead. In less than a minute they were on top.

"Stay down!" commanded the foreman.

Looking out across the prairie, they could see that the five riders had abandoned the ten steers. They were galloping furiously to the south. Upset and angry at her foreman and the thieves, Elizabeth raised her rifle, aimed and fired. The distance was over four hundred yards and increasing. The woman fired over and over, levering shells into her rifle. Then, the rustlers disappeared into an arroyo.

"Why did you stop me!" shouted Elizabeth. "No wonder we lose cattle! You're too afraid to stand and fight!"

For the first time since she had met Chappy Blue, she saw him lose control. He put down his rifle. With hands of steel he clenched tightly around Elizabeth's upper arms and squeezed hard. The man's eyes blazed and his darkly tanned face turned to a bronzed hue.

"If anything happened to you when those rustlers were shooting, I could never have lived with myself," he said in a tone of voice she had never heard him use.

The foreman was visibly upset, and he shook Elizabeth's arms for emphasis while his hands squeezed tighter and tighter.

"If you think me a coward, then fire me. Because boss lady, I don't care what you think. Truth be told, I'm glad they're gone cause a bullet from one of their rifles don't care if you're a man or a woman."

"But we could have shot back," said Elizabeth. "They got away, and now we won't…"

Chappy bent down and picked up his rifle. With careless and angry abandon, the cowboy slid and climbed down the steep hill to his horse. Elizabeth stared back at her foreman, then she switched holds on her rifle as she tried to massage away the pain in her arms.

At the base of the hill, the foreman mounted. He rode to the black, leaned over, grabbed reins, and sat unmoving while he waited. Elizabeth eventually came down off the hill. She put away her rifle, then pushed a left foot into a stirrup and rose up on her saddle. Chappy tossed reins, and she caught them. One leather strap slapped across her left cheek, causing a sharp pain. Her foreman simply turned his horse and headed back along the trail. He remained far in the lead, making any type of conversation impossible. She stared at his back all the way to the ranch.

When he rode up to the corral, Chappy dismounted and tied reins. Without waiting for her, the foreman walked to his private room. By the time Elizabeth reached the corral fence, dismounted, and tied her horse, Chappy was back. He was carrying a large bag and full saddlebags. He went to his horse. At that moment, Shorty came out of the cook shack, flour on his arms and one cheek, wearing a short white hat.

"What's up, Chappy?" asked Shorty. "You're back early."

The foreman told Shorty about the rustlers and the boss's actions during the altercation. Then he turned to Miss Elizabeth.

"Ma'am," said Chappy firmly. "Maybe in a few days, when that friend of Blanche's arrives, you can hire him to lead this bunch of misfits."

"Where are you going?" asked Elizabeth, wide-eyed and astonished.

At that moment, Blanche and George Temple came out of the house and walked towards the group standing in front of the cook shack.

"I quit," said Chappy loud enough for everyone present to hear.

"But why?" exclaimed Elizabeth. "I admit I was angry but it was the heat of the moment. You don't need to quit over…"

"Thought for a time that I could work for a boss lady. But I see I was wrong. Corralling a headstrong woman from back East is not my style. You may be the owner, but there can only be one foreman giving the orders. You're too bull-headed and I can't work for you. Sooner or later you'll put yourself in danger you can't get out of, and I couldn't live with that."

"But Chappy," pleaded Elizabeth. "I need you. Not only to boss the crew but to help with the plans for the ranch, and…"

"I already told you what you needed to know. Maybe that Larry fellow can follow through. You don't want a man who thinks for himself; you made that plain. What you need is some feller to follow your orders, even when they're wrong, and it's not me."

All the time he was speaking he was busy tying saddlebags to the cantle. The large round canvas bag he threw up on the horse and then mounted, balancing the bag before him.

"Don't quit, Chappy," said Elizabeth. "The men here want you, and I need you."

"In case you're wondering," said the man, "this horse is mine, bought and paid for."

Tipping a right hand to his sombrero, Chappy saluted everyone present. Then, holding the large bag across the pommel with his left and taking reins with his right, the former foreman turned the horse and kicked spurs into its sides. The mustang lurched forward into a trot, and dust rose under hooves as man and beast went up the road and towards town.

"I'd say," said George Temple, making an annoying sucking sound with tongue against teeth. "That you lost a mighty good man there."

"Oh shut up, George!" declared Elizabeth in sudden anger.

Blanche, George, and Shorty, stood with frozen expressions as they watched in disbelief as Elizabeth stomped toward the house and disappeared through the front door. The three of them, each holding a hand to forehead against the sun's glare, stared off into the distance where Chappy Blue and his horse could still be seen growing smaller with each forward movement.

"The fellers sure ain't gonna' like this," declared Shorty.

CHAPTER 18

Millers Rock was a high hill with a jumble of large boulders and solid granite at its top. Leonard Newton had purchased a shotgun for the occasion and came early. He left his horse picketed before him so he could keep an eye on it. When the mustang stopped grazing bits of grass, it raised its head to one direction and became alert. The former Easterner turned thief and killer knew the outlaw Jacob and his gang were approaching.

Five men rode up and dismounted next to the picketed horse. One of the outlaws took the reins of the five horses while Jake and three other men looked for the owner of the grounded mustang.

"I'm here," said Leonard, standing up and exposing head and shoulders from behind rock.

The twin barrels of the shotgun could easily be seen resting upon a stone and pointing skyward.

"I see you brought backup," said Jake. "If we wanted to get you, that popgun won't stop us. It has limited range."

"Let's just say I don't like being unprepared," replied the scheming killer.

"All right, we're here. Now spill it."

"You're familiar with the Double TJ Ranch?"

One of the outlaws laughed, and Jake and the other men smiled.

"We're familiar," replied Jacob.

"No doubt you rustled cattle off their range?"

"We ain't saying," replied the leader. "But I will tell you we know that ranch is closed in on three sides by mountains in the back and by hills on each side."

"Do you know a trail where men could get in and out without being seen?"

"We might," replied Jacob. "What about the place?"

"Three weeks ago, two women from the East moved in. They call themselves the Grahams and go by the names of Blanche and Elizabeth. They claim to be the owners."

"Tell us something we don't know."

The men behind Jacob laughed.

"I saw them last Saturday at the dance," said Leonard.

"You and every single man in the county," said Jacob. "Real pretty, both of them. What about it?"

"Blanche is Elizabeth's hired traveling companion. They aren't cousins and Graham is not Elizabeth's real name."

"Go on."

"Never mind what her real name is," said Leonard. "But Elizabeth traveled under a false name to hide the fact that she's rich. Comes from a family of wealthy New Yorkers. Her father recently died and left her millions."

"How does that come into play?" asked Jacob.

"I want your men to kidnap her."

"Out here, men don't mess with women," said Jacob angrily. "Not if they don't want to rile a hornet's nest. If a fellow was stupid enough to take one, every man in the county who could tote a gun would be looking. Count us out."

"But you haven't heard all of my plan," said Leonard.

"Should have known better than to meet some dude from back East," clipped Jacob. "We're leaving."

"But there's big money in this," responded Leonard.

"There's not enough money in the world that would keep a man safe out here for molesting or bothering a woman," repeated Jacob. "You'd be wise to know that."

The outlaws walked back to their horses, grabbed reins, and mounted. With a shout and pressure of spurs, the five men galloped away.

"What a bunch of cowardly dumb clucks," said Leonard out loud and added a string of profane words.

I guess I'll have to hire men who'll take money, no questions asked, he thought.

CHAPTER 19

Hours after Chappy, her foreman, quit, Elizabeth was too upset to eat supper. She suffered from a tight and upset stomach. Going to the corral, she roped Salty and saddled him. The young boss led him to a water trough, let him drink, mounted, put spurs to the horse's sides, and rode away in a clatter.

George Temple, Shorty, and Jack rushed out of the cook house.

"I'll have to go after her," said George. "You watch Blanche."

"No, I'll go," said Jack. "That lady can ride, and George, you're not up to it."

Jack had his horse hitched in front, and he mounted and rode off, creating a string of dust that remained in the dry, windless air for some time.

Salty, constantly prodded by spurs, ran as he had never run before. Given loose reins, the mustang held its head high and pounded across the hard ground toward the southern range. Rider and horse came to a deep, wide arroyo. In complete rejection of caution, Elizabeth forced her mount to plunge down and across the deeply eroded scar in the land. Then, with great speed, she pushed her mount up its other steep side and onto the flat prairie.

It'll take time, but if I keep on, I'll find the place where the rustlers were, she thought. *Serve Chappy Blue right if I run into them again. What does he care what happens? How could he just up and leave when I needed...*

Elizabeth, bent over in the saddle behind the horse's neck and suddenly quit spurring. Salty, now at its limit, began to slow down. Eventually, the mount came to a trot and then to a walk. All tension on the reins was released, and the horse, sensing the rider's change in mood, came to a complete stop. The steed hung its head to blow and catch its wind.

Jack came over a rise, galloping furiously, worried over the lady boss and wondering what he would tell the other fellers if something happened to her. Since the foreman was gone, who was in charge? Who would he or the men turn to for direction? Then he saw her below on open grassland. Her horse was stopped, and she was bent over, shoulders shaking, and it was obvious she was crying. Jack, sure that he could protect her, pulled his mount to a quick stop and remained where he was.

"So she's just like any other woman," said Jack to his horse, patting its neck. "Bet it's Chappy that's making her all upset. Serves her right for chasing him away, ain't that right, boy?"

A scrub cedar tree was close to Jack, and he guided the horse behind it. Now hidden from view, he observed and guarded over the boss lady.

"Oh, you dumb, stupid fool!" blurted out Elizabeth.

The black she was sitting on was now standing out on the open prairie; the wind had begun to pick up. The rumbling of distant thunder was gradually growing louder as clouds from the west rushed over the mountains and began to blot out the blue sky. In her anger and self castigation, Elizabeth had paid no attention. Jack, who sat his horse high up on a hill looked down on his boss and began to worry. The storm was coming fast. Already the sky was completely overcast, and now lower clouds were rushing in. A mist of rain was beginning and thunder was growing louder. To the west, gray clouds turned to a darker hue, almost black. Rain at any time was rare, but this storm looked to be a bad one. Worse, between Elizabeth and Jack, was a deep arroyo.

A crack of loud thunder and then a downpour of rain instantly brought Elizabeth to awareness of her surroundings. From a hilltop, she heard gunfire, and she looked over and saw Jack racing down towards her, pistol held in his right hand and still firing. He came to a sliding stop at the bottom of the hill and before the deep wash. The rain was coming down so hard that the droplets pelting her clothing actually hurt.

“Miss Elizabeth!” shouted Jack. “Get across this wash before you’re stranded!”

She grabbed reins and guided Salty towards the arroyo.

“Leave the horse and climb down—run across to me!” shouted Jack.

Elizabeth pretended she didn’t hear him and rode along the steep wash, looking for a place to ride down. Jack followed her, shouting furiously words she could no longer hear. The downpour increased with a fury she did not believe possible. The rain came with such force she could barely see.

Jumping down, Elizabeth pulled the reins forward and led the horse toward the steep incline. A narrow ledge ran sideways, and she began to walk toward it. Already, the adobe had turned to thick, greasy clay, and clumps of it adhered to Elizabeth's boots, and she slipped and slid. Salty neighed loudly in complaint and pulled backward, jerking Elizabeth off her feet and onto her back. The hard fall took the wind from her. She heard Jack still shouting but couldn't make out his words. The rain gushed from the sky and blinded her.

Getting to her feet, she held the reins and pulled hard to get Salty to follow. Again, the horse neighed, pulled back hard, and again Elizabeth fell onto her back. This time, she lost her grip on the leather straps and slid down the steep incline into the wash. Landing feet first, she tripped, fell to her knees, and was covered in thick, sticky clay. She looked thirty feet across the wash to see Jack. Her vision was obscured but she thought Jack was holding a rope and he was still shouting frantically.

Turning, she looked up twenty feet and saw Salty standing and looking down. She tried to climb back up towards him, and all she could accomplish was to slide backward. Water, inches deep, was flowing over her boots.

"Elizabeth!" screamed Jack. "Run to me! Hurry!"

Not wanting to leave her horse, again Elizabeth tried to climb up the muddy slope. Again she slipped back and fell to her knees. Then came a terrific roar, an unusual sound she had never heard before. Looking up the wash, she saw a roiling wall of water, more than ten feet high.

"Run!" shouted Jack.

Elizabeth could barely hear the cowboy, but this time, she came to her feet and ran with all her might towards him. Looking to the west, she saw that she was going to be too late; the mass of water was nearly upon her. Then she felt something across her back. Jack stood above her, and holding the rope, he brought it tight around her shoulders and then one-handedly held it while he ran to his horse. Putting foot into stirrup, he jumped onto the saddle and wrapped his rope around the pommel. Urging his mount forward, Elizabeth was jerked from her feet as the wall of water rushed towards her.

Thoroughly drenched, she was struck hard with liquid sand and mud, she felt the force of the

Chapter 19

deluge. The raging torrent pulled at her as the rope constricted her with pain. She was at the very edge of the roiling silt. The two forces held her, pulling in different directions. Then she flew sideways and up and found herself being dragged across solid ground. Jack jumped off his horse and came running back to her.

"Are you hurt?" yelled Jack, pulling the rope from her shoulders.

Elizabeth was spitting dirt from her mouth and trying to clear her eyes. She coughed, and rain began to wash her hair and body clear of the mud and silt. The cowboy was beginning to realize she wasn't seriously hurt. It was a miracle and they both knew it.

"Just like catching a trout," declared Jack, who remained on bended knees and laughed in relief.

"Oh Jack," said Elizabeth. "You saved my life."

"By a hair's breadth, I'd say," beamed Jack once more. "And my pleasure, Miss Elizabeth. Wait until I tell the boys about this."

As quickly as the rain began, it stopped. Except for the maelstrom that raced past them in the wash, the sudden quiet was deafening. Already, the clouds were breaking up, and the blue sky and rays of sunlight were shining through.

"What about Salty?" asked Elizabeth, still lying on the wet muddy ground. "How will we get him across?"

"That fool horse was smarter than you, boss. He wasn't going down that wash with that wall of water coming. And I'm sure the horse is all right, probably in the shelter of those trees yonder."

As Jack said this, the saddled black appeared on the open prairie.

"There he is," said Jack.

The cowboy helped Elizabeth to her feet.

"Where is he?" asked the lady boss, pushing muddy hair out of her eyes.

Elizabeth found a soggy handkerchief in her pocket, but when she tried to wipe her face, coarse sandy grit abraded, and she stopped.

"Open your eyes," said Jack. "He's over there."

The wash in front of them was roaring with brown, muddy water.

"Oh, I see him," said Elizabeth. "How will we get him across?"

"We won't," said Jack. "It'll take quite a while for the wash to clear. And we're not going anywhere either. The ground is wet adobe; if we tried to move across it, we'd build up so much mud that we sure wouldn't get far. We'll have to wait and hope the sun dries the land out. But I think it's no good. We'll have to spend the night."

"Oh," said Elizabeth. "Whatever will they think back at the ranch?"

"Same as everyone else caught in this storm. That the ground turned to clay and we can't make it back."

"But Blanche and George and…will worry."

"You bet the whole outfit will fret. Can't be helped. Every cowhand will look for you as soon as anyone can travel."

"What will we do until…tomorrow?" asked the very wet lady, beginning to shiver.

"First thing is to get you out of those wet clothes," said Jack.

"But I couldn't…"

Jack laughed.

"No need to worry. I got my bedroll and an extra shirt and pants in my saddlebags. I'll lay the tarp down; you can undress under the blanket and get into my extra duds. They'll be good and dry all wrapped up. While you're doing that, I'll try to gather firewood. It'll be wet, but I'll get something going."

"Thank you, Jack," said Elizabeth, trying to smile and still attempting to wipe grit from her face and eyes. "Thank you again for saving my life and… watching out after me."

"My pleasure, Miss Elizabeth," replied Jack. "And maybe you learned your lesson about riding off like that. This ain't New York City; this is the honest-to-goodness wild West, and out here, a grown man can lose his life in a minute. Never know what man, beast, or thing will raise its ugly head and bite your face off. I'm sure you learned a good lesson."

Elizabeth, still wide-eyed and shaken, felt miserable in her wet condition. This time she did not answer Jack. But when he laid out the tarp, she eagerly scampered onto the clean surface and immediately began taking off her wet boots. When she was handed the blanket and dry clothing, she covered herself, shivering uncontrollably now, and waited for Jack to wander off in search of wood.

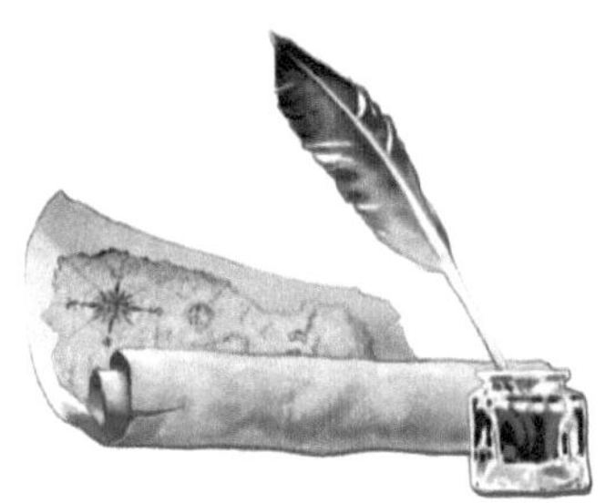

CHAPTER 20

Frustrated that he could not convince Jacob and his gang to follow his plan, Leonard Newton began to frequent other saloons. It did not take long to find one close to the brothels whose patrons were as unsavory a form of low life that could be found anywhere in the West. These were men that one did not want to meet in the dark and who would kill another man for a few silver coins.

Leonard himself was reverting to a type. Despite his upbringing and education, the very atmosphere of few social standards and very little law brought out the worst in the man. Changing his clothes to that of a Westerner allowed the former Easterner to relax all inner inhibitions he had ever harbored or had forced upon him. In his cabin, he began to sleep the morning through, rose in the afternoon, splashed a little water on his face, brushed his teeth, and then searched for a restaurant or saloon that served food. Being bored and having money, he gambled and having learned a few skills with cards others did not have, he won often. Sometimes, men challenged him, and Leonard was always ready with the derringer. He had been out West only a little while, yet he managed to provoke and wound four men over cards. So far, none of these episodes had involved the law. How different it would have been back East. Leonard was beginning to enjoy himself and let loose with his inner desires. He enjoyed shooting these scum that he felt were hardly worth the price of the bullets he used on them.

Leonard awoke around noon. Today, he resolved that he would find men to help him pull off his plan, and nothing was going to stop him. Enough time had gone by and he wasn't delaying any longer. Getting up, he washed, dressed, and looked at himself in a cracked mirror. His beard was growing untrimmed and so was his hair. After a meal, he would seek a barber; some time that evening, he would find and hire the men he needed.

Leonard treated himself and went to a hotel restaurant for steak and lobster with a bottle of good imported wine. The meal cost him, but he had the money, and he didn't care. From now on, one way or the other, he would always have money. Walking down the street, he came to a barber who advertised shaves, haircuts, and various hair tonics. Leonard walked in, and there was a man in the barber chair getting a shave and another waiting. The place had a strong scent about it, not altogether unpleasant.

"You sit, Mister," said the barber in a German accent, holding a razor with lather and looking up from his work. "Be vith you, after that...other fellow."

The barber went back to shaving his customer and, when finished, splashed something sweet-smelling on the man's face. The customer paid and the other man got up and took a seat. A conversation between the next patron and the barber took place, but Leonard paid no attention. What he did notice was that the barber used the same towel on the man as he had used on the previous patron. Shaking his head in disgust, Leonard sat and looked at the framed pictures of Western scenes on the wall and at various advertisements. Bored, he picked up an old newspaper some customer had brought in from some other location. He glanced at its front page and idly read without taking any real interest. "The Delta Independent Vol.VI Tuesday, August 21, 1888. NO. 26."

"Mister," called the barber. "You next."

Leonard got up and took a seat.

"Wass vork you vish?" asked the hair trimmer.

"If you know what's good for you, you'll use a clean towel on me."

"Yeah?"

"I said a clean towel."

"Cost extra."

"Put a dirty towel anywhere on me, and I'll shoot your ears off."

"Nein, sir!" replied the barber. "Ahh, yeah, neu Gesichtstuch. Ahh, a towel!"

Thoroughly nervous to be threatened, the barber reached for a clean towel and held it so the man with the cold black eyes could see.

"Your pleasure, sir?" asked the immigrant barber in his clipped accent.

"I want my beard trimmed and my hair cut," said Leonard. "See to it, you do a good job."

"Yeah, I do good vork."

With a shaking hand, the barber began to trim the customer's beard, relieved that he did not ask for a shave. When he was finished trimming the beard, the barber held up a small round mirror so his customer could survey the work. The barber sensed this was a thoroughly bad man and wanted to take no chances. The man with the dark piercing eyes examined himself.

"Here," said Leonard. "Cut more off the bottom and sides, and trim the mustache closer."

"Yeah, vill do...sir!"

With each passing moment the German barber was becoming more and more nervous. Since opening the barbershop a year before, he never had a customer who affected him the way this one did. Being a people person he had some clairvoyant perception of this newcomer, information about this hard man the barber wished he did not possess. A cruel and mean persona emanated from the man, which made the barber shake even more while using his scissors. Finished with the beard and showing his work once again, the barber moved on to cutting the man's dark hair.

Leonard sensed the man's nervousness and took delight in his discomfiture. Several times the barber had to stop and take deep breaths. He was sweating now from an uncommon fear that suddenly gripped him. Holding his right hand with his left, he tried to relax the arm and stop it from shaking.

"Hurry, man!" shouted Leonard. "Quit lollygagging, I don't have all day to sit here."

The barber jumped with a terrific tremor that shook him from head to toe. This customer was driving him out of his mind with fear.

"Yeah…yeah…sir!" stammered the hair trimmer, his lips actually trembling as he spoke.

Leonard stared at the man and inwardly smiled at the quavering fellow and the fearful effect he was causing.

The barber tried to relax but couldn't. Now, his right hand was shaking madly, and he was awkwardly trying to hold it steady with his other hand. It was an odd and new way to cut hair, but he couldn't perform the task any other way. Slowly the haircut progressed. Time seemed endless, and sweat dripped from the barber's face and down into his eyes. Then, just before he finished, he slipped nervously, and the end of the shears cut into the customer's ear.

Leonard roared with the sharp pain of it, jumped from his chair and touched his ear. Blood came away on his right hand. Grabbing the little barber by his front apron, he was jerked forward, and Leonard, losing all control of himself, slapped the man back and forth with the flat of his right hand until the man begged him to stop. Blood began to trickle from the nose and mouth of the barber.

"Think I'm finished?" shouted Leonard, still holding the man by his front.

Dragging the barber to the counter where combs, scissors, and other implements of the trade were kept, Leonard picked up a straight razor. The barber screamed loudly and began to plead for his life. The door of the little shop opened and a bell rang.

"What's going on here?" asked a man's voice.

"None of your business, Mister," shouted Leonard, still in a rage and attempting to open the straight razor in his hand.

"Let that man go!" came the reply.

"You'll stay out of this, if you know what's good for you. This fool of a man cut me and I'm going to cut him back."

There was the distinct click of a revolver hammer being pulled back, and with that sound, Leonard came to his senses, his rage subsiding somewhat as he turned to look at a tall man wearing a deputy sheriff badge and holding a cocked pistol in his right hand. Leonard dropped the unopened razor to the floor.

"That's better," said the deputy. "Now pay the barber and get out. If I catch you doing any more mischief, I'll shoot first and ask questions later."

"Who are you?" asked Leonard, his anger now transferred to the lawman.

"If you must know, the name's Chappy Blue, lawman. Looks like I arrived just in time."

"So you understand, copper," sneered Leonard. "This fool of a barber cut my ear, and I got riled. Any man would. He doesn't deserve to be paid, but here's two bits, twice the going rate."

Leonard took a quarter from his pocket and threw it up in the air. It fell back with a clatter to the wooden floor and rolled. Then Leonard walked out the door. The barber collapsed back in his chair; taking up the towel, he wiped at the blood dripping from his nose and bruised face.

"Tank...you...deputy," exclaimed the barber. "Mein Gott! I tink he vass going to kill me. That's baddest man to come to my shop. Makes me tink to quit."

"Before you do," replied Chappy Blue. "You mind giving me a haircut and a shave?"

"It vould be my pleasure," beamed the barber, wincing at the pain it caused him. "And no charge for you."

"Never mind that," said Chappy. "Just glad to be of service."

“That man vould haff killed me sure,” said the barber, fetching a clean towel for the deputy. “I know he vould have cut me something awful.”

“What’s his name?” asked Chappy.

“I asked customer about him vhen I first saw stranger come to town. I have knack on names. His first ist Leonard. He’s card sharp in saloons. He shoots men over cards. Not pistole, little gun. Real sneaky fellow.”

“I’ll talk to the town marshall about him. See that he’s watched. No fellow should lose his temper like that man did.”

“I got look in eyes,” said the barber. “Man dead inside! Man crazy!”

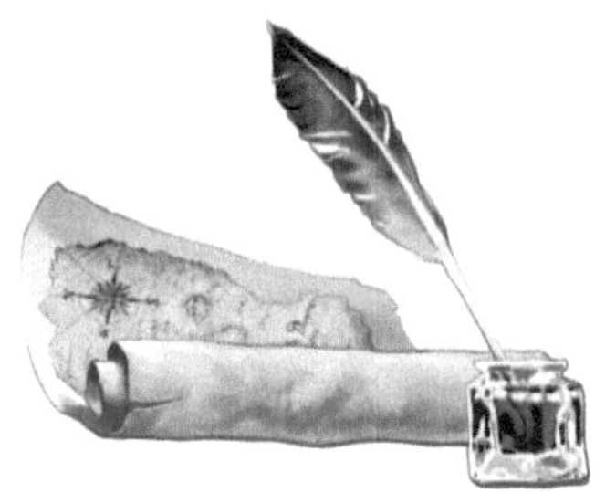

CHAPTER 21

"Morning, Miss Elizabeth," called out Jack. "For breakfast we have rabbit and water."

Under the blanket, Elizabeth had shivered and slept in fits. The temperature had dropped into the forties, and she had fallen into a deep sleep at some time in the morning. Now that she was fully awake, she felt feverish; her throat hurt, and her nose ran. She knew she would come down with a terrible ague.

"Oh Jack, how on earth did you sleep last night?" said Elizabeth, and then sneezed.

"I slept on pine boughs, had that and the horse blanket for cover, and my saddle for a pillow," said Jack. "How did you sleep, Miss Elizabeth?"

"I kept waking up. I was cold."

Jack handed Elizabeth a canteen and, on a stick, a quarter cut of a rabbit.

"No salt, and it'll be stringy and tough, but it's food."

"How did you catch it?" she asked.

"With a snare. Been doing that since I was a kid. Soon as you eat, we'll ride back to the ranch. The ground is drying up, and we should not have much trouble."

"What about catching Salty?"

"I already crossed over and got him. Fit as a fiddle is that hoss. Now, Miss Elizabeth, I want to ask if you'll play along when we get back."

"Yes?"

"I've been lorded over by the likes of Rusty, Shorty, and the boys for many years now. But if you let me tell the story of how I saved your life from that raging torrent and…well…the boys will be green that it was me that done it. If you'll play along and build me up as your hero, it'll make me plumb proud. I want a chance to make those fellers suffer like they made me all these years."

"Why Jack, you did save me, and if it wasn't for what you did, I'd be… Anyway, every time I woke up, I shivered at the thought of what would have happened if you had missed with your lasso. You *are* my hero, Jack, and you just go ahead and tell your friends any way you want. There are not enough words to tell you how grateful I am."

Salty acted eager to see his rider. For the first time the black actually nuzzled Elizabeth while she saddled him. They rode slowly across the prairie, Jack trying his best to ride over rocky ground and avoid the wet and soft places. It took twice as long to get near the ranch, and as they came over a rise, they were met on the drying prairie by Shorty, Rusty, Lefty, and a number of other riders.

"Miss Elizabeth, we're sure glad to see you!" exclaimed Shorty.

"Where in tarnation you been, Jack?" asked Rusty. "You git lost or something?"

"Miss Elizabeth got caught up in a flood down in that deep wash yonder. I come up on her just in time. I threw my loop as she rose up ridin' the top of the first wave and me and my hoss fished her across and out of the bubbling mess. Just like she was a trout. I'm her hero, boys. Ain't that the gosh almighty truth of it, Miss Elizabeth?"

"Aww, you fib, Jack," said Rusty.

"You always stretched the truth, Jack," said Shorty. "I don't believe…"

"Every word he says is the gospel truth," interjected Elizabeth, attempting to speak the lingo.

"See!" beamed Jack. "I saved the boss, and I'm her genuine hero!"

As they rode back to the ranch, Jack expounded on his rescue, and when one of the men questioned a particular point, Jack deferred to the boss lady, and she corroborated his story. When they arrived at the ranch, the exhausted ranch owner attempted to remove tack, but between her coughing and sneezing, she lacked the energy. When Rusty insisted on performing the task, she acquiesced and excused herself to go back to the house to clean up and rest.

George Temple and Blanche met Elizabeth at the door, and they demanded to know what happened. Elizabeth collapsed in a chair and gave a brief explanation, and then she began a fit of coughing, followed by several large sneezes.

"Oh! You get out of those old clothes," said Blanche. "George and I will heat water for the tin tub. You'll take a hot bath and go directly to bed."

Elizabeth was, for once, too tired and sick to resist their help. She went to her bedroom and lay down. It wasn't long and the two of them carried in the tub. After some time, pails and pots of hot water were brought to fill the vessel. Elizabeth enjoyed the hot soak and, changing into bed clothes, she tiredly got between clean sheets and fell asleep. When she awoke, she found a tray of coffee and a plate of bacon and eggs. The exhausted young woman drank the coffee, finished the food, and immediately fell back to sleep. Her last thought was of Chappy, his words, and how grateful she was to be alive.

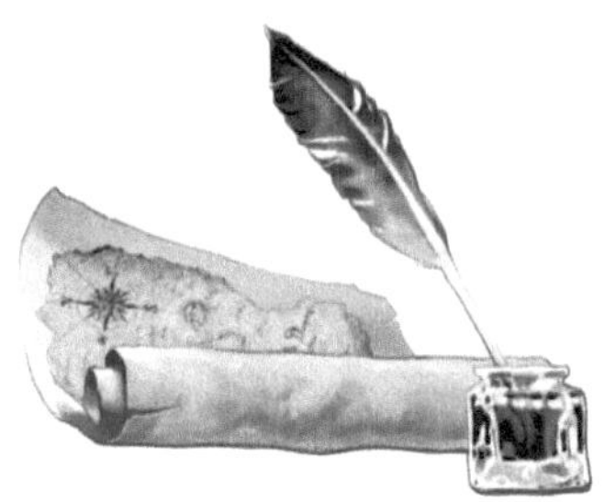

CHAPTER 22

Chappy Blue took it upon himself to investigate rustling. Unlike other lawmen, being the past foreman of the Double TJ Ranch, the new deputy had a special interest in stopping cattle theft for good. It was his way to interview all witnesses and speak to the owners. Like that fellow who was accosting the barber, there were many unsavory characters around Golden, Colorado. Top on the list was Jacob and his gang. Chappy was sure that several groups were rustling cattle, and so far, they had been very good at getting in and away with the steers. They planned their raids on Sundays and odd times when men would most likely be away from the stock. And, they only took a few at a time, making it easier to move and sell without being caught.

The talk with the local marshal revealed that the full name of the man at the barbershop was Leonard Newton, and he was some fellow from back East. He bought a little shack and some land without any visible means of support. The man was spending his nights playing poker and winning more than losing. The marshal explained the fellow backed his wins with a derringer. So far, the wounded men involved did not go to the law.

"Sooner or later he's going to kill a man," explained the marshal. "When he does, I'll be there to put on the irons. I don't like men who carry a hide-out gun and who cheat at cards."

***

Chappy went back to the jail. With his new job, he hadn't had time to find a room, so temporarily he was staying in a cell. His thoughts went back to the ranch and the men he had bossed. He missed the range, and he really did care about what happened to the Double TJ, its hands, and the new owners. Those fellows were a good bunch, and Shorty's cooking couldn't be topped. Then despite his iron will, that girl intruded into his thinking.

Not in a million years had he ever thought he would meet in the flesh someone who was actually prettier than those pictures he saw of society ladies or models in magazines. Not only was she attractive, but she was educated. But there were some problems with her common sense and her strong will that he could not handle. Not that he approved of any woman wearing the pants. And, there was something fishy. Blanche was nothing like her cousin.

If they really are cousins, Chappy thought. *And... what do I know about women anyway? But, to top it off, Elizabeth can ride as good as any man, maybe even better. And does she have spunk. She sure gave that bucking bronc a long turn or two. A real little muscular wisp of a thing. Too brave for her own good. And at the dance she handled those men so cleverly. That dress she wore took every feller's breath away. No matter how much I care, I won't let no Eastern gal boss me. What am I thinking? A fancy woman like that wouldn't take any interest in me anyway. Best I left when I did.*

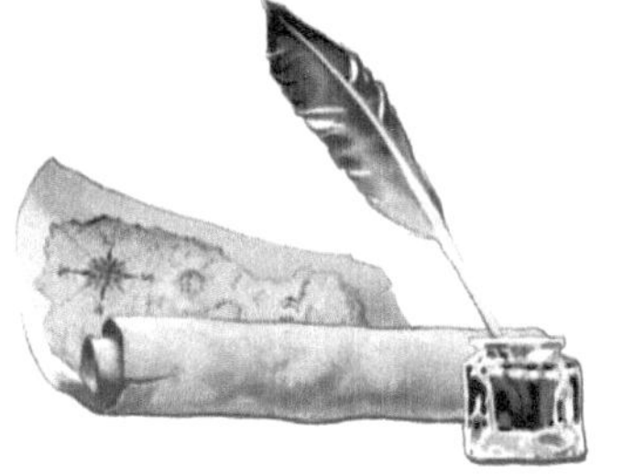

CHAPTER 23

Larry Roth came on the fourth Saturday in October and Blanche Graham, George Temple, Jack, and Rusty met him at the train station.

"Larry!" gushed Blanche when he walked up to her on the platform.

"Blanche!" exclaimed Larry Roth.

George, Jack, and Rusty were invisible as far as the greeting between Blanche and Larry was concerned. The meeting between them was like lost lovers in their actions and their emotions. If two people were made for each other, this pair was it. They stared in unbroken silence. Their hands clasped together, Larry bent down from his great height and kissed Blanche on the cheek.

"I dreamed of this moment," said Larry simply.

"Me, too," declared Blanche. "How good of you to keep your promise."

Jack, Rusty, and George rolled their eyes and stood by waiting. The silence continued, seemingly unendingly, as the man and woman stared at each other without embarrassment.

"Say!" began Jack. "How about if we go to the horses. Larry, we picked out a spirited mustang for you, and so's you know, my names Jack, and this is my pard Rusty, and that there feller is George."

"Glad to meet ya," said Larry, breaking his reverie and shaking hands with the men. "I've met George before. Where's Miss Elizabeth?"

"She's home sick," said Blanche.

"That's too bad," responded Larry. "Did she get caught in the rain or something?"

Rusty and George groaned because they knew what was coming next.

"Well, Larry, old fellow," began Jack. "I got a little story to tell you about that."

Jack, well rehearsed now, began a long-winded tale of how he saved the boss lady from the raging torrent in the wash. He began to talk and before he finished, the five riders were miles past town and well on their way to the ranch.

"Now that's a story to be heard!" said Larry. "Jack, I especially liked the part where pulling Miss

Elizabeth out of the wash was just like catching a trout. Did she get injured?"

"She was wet and cold and caught the ague," said Blanche, finding a chance to interrupt and a bit perturbed at Jack for usurping the moment.

When they arrived at the ranch, Jack carried the newcomer's bag to the room of the previous foremen. In Chappy's absence, Blanche had decorated the room with Indian blankets, rugs on the floor, and various Western artwork she put on the walls, thinking it would make the place more comfortable. After showing Larry Roth his room, they went to the cook shack for coffee and food. They found Elizabeth there and waiting for them.

"You shouldn't be out of bed," declared Blanche.

"I've been confined for three days now. I can only stand so much pampering. Besides, I'm better, thanks to Shorty's soups and remedies."

Shorty smiled and nodded his head.

"It's good to see you, Larry," said Elizabeth. "I trust you had a good trip."

"I did," responded the cowboy. "I'm sorry you've been ill. Thank you for allowing me to come."

"Lizzy," began Blanche. "We just showed Larry his room. We were going to visit you after lunch so you and he could discuss your plans."

"Miss Elizabeth," said Larry. "Jack told me about your adventure. Sounds like you're very lucky to be here."

"Indeed. It does look like I have a great deal more to learn about living out here. I've taken notes on various aspects of the ranch that I would like to discuss with you. But first, it might be best if you and I take a ride so you can see for yourself what I'm talking about."

"I think that would be a good start," replied Larry. "Blanche, will you be going with us?"

"I would like to, but I'm afraid my riding skills are limited," she replied. "As much as I want to, I would just hold you up and be in the way."

After lunch, Jack, Larry, and Elizabeth set out on a ride southwest towards the mountains to look over the several canyons and potential places for dams. They spent the rest of the day riding and came back for a late supper. Blanche waited anxiously for their return, and she and Larry spent the evening walking and talking before turning in.

For the next several days, starting after breakfast, Jack, acting as temporary foreman, Elizabeth, and Larry explored the ranch. When that was completed, they sat in the office, went over a map of the ranch, and laid out potential plans for dams, catch ponds, and irrigation.

"Before I left, I wrote down the name of an engineer we used," said Larry. "If you want, we could send for him, or you could pick out someone else."

"Do you and your father trust this man?"

"Yes, he has worked for us on several projects."

"Then you can go to town and send a wire."

"Miss Elizabeth," said Larry. "We haven't discussed this, but it'll cost some money to bring the engineer here and a whole lot more to construct those dams and irrigation ditches. I could help a little if you need it, but I'm afraid it'll cost more than what I…"

"That's very generous of you, Larry," replied Elizabeth. "I have an uncle back in New York, and he has already told me he will loan us the necessary funds."

"Good!" replied Larry. "Then I'll go to town first thing tomorrow and send a wire."

The initial plans were complete; Larry spent the remaining days with Blanche, and the two of them went off on private rides and picnics. Sometimes, Elizabeth accompanied them, and other times, she rode with Jack. Both were giving the hands daily ranch duties. Despite Jack's and George Temple's warnings, there were times when Elizabeth would get ahead or behind them or leave altogether without telling anyone and go explore the ranch on her own.

If anyone loved horses, and horseback riding, it was Elizabeth. She loved the Western saddle. The large leather seat added to the enormous pleasure of riding. Despite her dangerous experience, she still didn't seem to learn. Fear, was not a part of Miss Elizabeth 'Lizzy' Burnett's nature.

CHAPTER 24

For a week Leonard Newton scouted the Double TJ Ranch. He discovered a rundown nester's cabin in the hills to the south, not far from the main spread. He moved supplies into the cabin and began using it. With a spyglass, he carefully looked over the ranch Elizabeth claimed to inherit. He began to track movement of men and cattle. Eventually, he discovered Elizabeth's routine. She left the ranch in the mornings and took one of two trails. One led to the canyons in the south, and the other to where the cattle were grazing. With the information Leonard gathered, he felt he was ready. He went to town and paid five rough characters to meet him at two o'clock at Millers Rock.

That afternoon, five bearded and very tough-looking men rode up to the isolated crag. Horses were tied and the men dismounted. Leonard Newton was in the rocks, holding a shotgun and waiting for them.

"All right, find a seat and hear what I have to say," said Leonard, sitting down on Millers Rock.

The five unsavory characters came closer and sat down.

"What's the mystery?" asked one. "You gave us fifty bucks each and told us to meet here. What you got on your mind?"

"I'm asking you to take my orders. Any man not willing to do that can leave now."

The five looked at each other.

"What orders?" asked a man with a deep scar across his face.

"I'm paying each one of you three hundred dollars in gold to do a job. Half now, and the other half when completed."

"That's a lot of money," said one of the fellows.

"What you want us to do?" asked another.

"Once I tell you," said Leonard, "none of you can leave."

"For that kind of money, I'm in," replied one man.

"Heck, for that kind of money," said the fellow with the scar, "I'm willing to do most anything."

This was followed by the assent of the other four.

"Good," said Leonard.

One outlaw made a deep-throated cough, another lit a cigarette, and a third grimaced.

"How many of you are familiar with the Double TJ Ranch?"

"We all are," said one of the men.

"And everyone knows about the two pretty ladies from back East," said another.

"What I hired you five for is to grab the one named Elizabeth and take her to that empty nester's shack south of this place. I…"

"That's a fool's job," said one of the roughians. "Grab one of those women, and there'd be an army out looking. They'd shoot first and ask questions later."

The man stood up and started to leave.

"Stop!" called Leonard. "I told you, no one leaves…"

He cocked both hammers of the double barrel shotgun and aimed it at the man. The outlaw turned, bent low while reaching for his pistol. Leonard Newton pulled the triggers and buckshot tore into the deserter. He screamed with pain and then fell face forward, dead. Leonard pulled his pistol and cocked it.

"Anyone else going to back out?"

The four men shook their heads and Leonard lowered the hammer and holstered his .38 Colt.

"That's better. Now let's go over my plans. With one man dead, the price just went up. I'll pay the rest of you three hundred fifty each. It's a simple job, I'm asking. You grab the lady while she's out on the range and bring her to the nester's shack. When you take Elizabeth, you don't hurt any part of that woman. You simply gag her, tie her up, and bring her to me. Then you men can go on your way."

"What if we run into trouble?"

"Make sure there is none," replied Leonard. "If you're careful and grab her and get away without anyone seeing, then all you have to do is mess up your tracks."

"When do we do this here job?" asked the man with the scar.

"I'm paying you to stay with me tonight at the nester's shack." With that statement Leonard threw down four sacks containing one-hundred-fifty dollars in gold. "I'll keep the fifth sack to divide up later."

"All right!" said the man with the scar, undoing the sack to see the money.

The other three did the same.

"So you know, I got food and supplies at the cabin. Tomorrow I'll divide the four of you and put you on two different trails Elizabeth rides. She always has an escort watching over her, but quite often she rides ahead. You either grab her when she's alone or, if you have to, kill the guard and take her."

"For this kind of money," said one of the men, "we'll get er done!"

"Good!" replied Leonard. "Besides, what else do you men have to do? We can talk more at the cabin. Before we go, you cover that man I shot with stones."

The four outlaws hesitated and, seeing no way out, did as they were told. When they were finished, they mounted. One of them took reins of the fifth horse. Leonard got on his mustang, holding his reloaded shotgun, and rode behind the hired thugs.

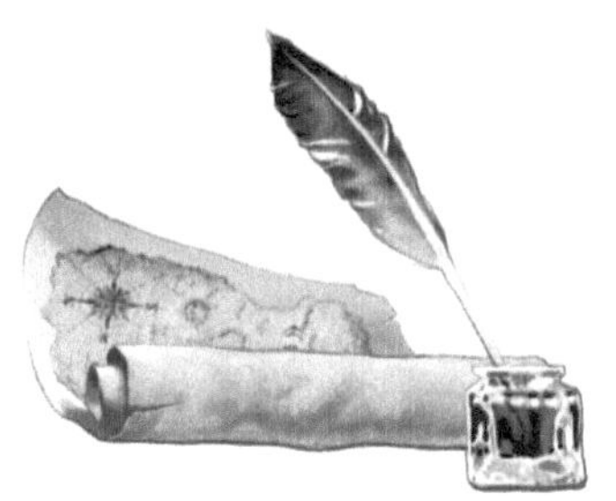

CHAPTER 25

"Blanche, after I help Miss Elizabeth and you with the ranch, will you come back with me to Kansas?" asked Larry Roth.

"Larry, I would love to, but Lizzy needs me to be her companion; I just can't abandon her…"

"Every time I ask you, the same answer comes from your lips. Don't you know how I care for you?"

"And I for you."

"The engineer came last night, and he and Jack are already looking at one of the canyons. Suppose you remain at the ranch today and decide what you are going to do."

It was their first real argument. Blanche watched as Larry caught a mustang, bridled and saddled him, and rode away. Elizabeth and George Temple came from the ranch house.

"We're going up to the canyon to meet the engineer," said Elizabeth. "Where's Larry?"

"We had a disagreement," replied her cousin, pointing. "He just rode away. I can still see him off in the distance."

Again Blanche watched as Elizabeth and George caught their horses and rode off. She walked about the courtyard, went to the cook shack, and sat down. Shorty came and brought a cup of coffee.

"Would like to stay and talk, but I got rolls to take from the oven," said the cook.

The young woman drank half a cup and then went back outside. She brooded over her decision, but the answer appeared to be an obvious one. No matter how loyal she should be to Elizabeth, she could no longer stay with her. The facts were evident. It was the rich young woman and her uncle who had saved her from an awful life. And, without their help she would have become homeless, or perhaps even worse. There was no denial, and this was a huge betrayal of trust. But still, eventually, she would have to leave Lizzy. She loved this man with all her heart and would not risk losing him. It would be hard, but she had to tell her boss she was going to quit her job and go with Larry.

The decision made, it was like a tremendous weight was lifted from her shoulders. Then, she had a sudden and immediate thought. If she could catch, bridle, and saddle her horse, she would ride to where Larry was and tell him of her decision.

It took several tries for Blanche to lasso her mustang. The horse finally gave up being chased around the corral and stood still for her. The need for speed gave her courage. Tying the rope to the hitching post, it took three fearful attempts before she got the bit past the teeth of the horse and in its proper place. Bridled, reins dangling, she tried throwing the saddle up over the blanket she had placed on the horse's back. She finally accomplished this task, worried that she had left a wrinkle to irritate the poor animal. The cowboys had told her a wrinkle could cause a sore. Pulling hard, she finally tightened the cinch and tied it off. Feeling she had done a good job of saddling her mount for the first time, she led it out of the corral and closed the gate. Then Blanche put left foot to left stirrup and climbed aboard. Smiling at her new found success, she rode off in the direction Larry had ridden.

***

It was that morning Leonard Newton, holding the shotgun, led the four men to where he had last seen Elizabeth riding.

"Two of you hide here," he ordered. "Sometimes she and a guard come this way. If she comes along and the guard is with her, kill him and take the woman. I gave two of you rope and cloth for a gag, and a sack to put over her head so she won't see where she's going.

"What if she sees our faces?" asked one of the kidnappers.

"You cover them with kerchiefs!" replied Leonard.

"What if they don't show?" asked the man with the scar.

"When it gets dark, come back to the cabin, and we'll try again tomorrow," snarled Leonard. "Listen, you four. What I'm asking you to do is not that hard. But it's important to me. When you return with the girl, I'll pay you the rest of the gold and you can be on your way."

"Right boss," said the fellow with the scar. "For that kind of money, we'll get it done."

"You other two come with me," said Leonard. "There's another trail she rides."

Two of the hired men took position behind brush and a large boulder. The other two followed Leonard. They traveled a short distance and stopped.

"Hide here and do the same as I told the others. Don't make any mistakes."

Leonard rode off, but he did not ride far. There was no trust with men such as these. He wasn't about to let them leave with the knowledge they now had. Riding up a hill he had previously picked out, he dismounted and tied his horse. Taking a spyglass from his saddlebags he sat down and waited. From this location he could see both trails. If Elizabeth was coming, it would be within the next two hours.

***

George Temple and Elizabeth should have been miles ahead and nearly to the canyon where the engineer was. But George's horse had reared up at something on the trail, and the bodyguard had fallen and injured his hip. He tried getting back on his horse, but the pain he suffered was too severe. He tried walking. Frustrated, Elizabeth had no choice but to dismount and walk beside her bodyguard.

"For a tough guy," said Elizabeth, "you sure let that horse defeat you."

"Sorry, but I'm afraid that horse is my 'Achilles heel'," replied George.

"I want to get there to meet the engineer Larry hired before he finishes looking at the canyon."

"I told you we should have gotten ready earlier," said George.

With that, the man couldn't go any further and sat down, holding his horse's reins.

***

Blanche tried her best to follow the fresh horse tracks. For a long distance it was no problem. It was when she came to the rocky ground and two trails intersected that she had trouble choosing which one to take. She chose the left, and it was the wrong one.

***

"Here comes someone!" said one of the kidnappers.

"Is it a woman?" asked the second outlaw.

"Looks like it, and she's alone."

Blanche did not know what happened, but a rope descended around her and she was pulled roughly from her horse. She hit the ground hard and on her right side. The derringer she carried fell out of her vest pocket and into the bushes. The woman was too dazed to scream and then she felt someone grab her from behind, tie her hands, place a cloth around her mouth, and then a bag descended over her head. Terrified, all she could do was struggle to breathe through her nose as best she could.

***

Nearly an hour later, George recovered enough to start walking. Elizabeth and her bodyguard slowly advanced up the trail, each holding their horses' reins. They traveled some distance, but the woman realized they would never reach the canyon with Larry, Jack, and the engineer on time. Then, the distinct sound of a rifle firing up the trail echoed across the land. Elizabeth turned to look back at her companion and she saw George slump and fall to the ground. His horse snorted and trotted off. She saw blood on the bodyguard's chest, and the way he hit the dirt, she felt certain it was a fatal wound. She let go of the reins of her horse and bent down to examine George. He was shot in the heart and was dead. Elizabeth pulled her derringer out, and then she felt a rope constrict around her chest, and she was yanked off her feet. Struggling, she turned to see two masked men run towards her, one still holding a rope. Behind her, Salty neighed and trotted away.

Elizabeth tried to rise and shoot, but the man pulled hard on the lasso, and she fell back. Then, one of the men pried the derringer from her grasp. Within moments the woman was tied, gagged, and a cloth sack covered her head. Still, she struggled.

"Hold steady," ordered a voice. "You ain't going nowhere."

Elizabeth continued to fight.

"Got a real she-cat," said one of the kidnappers, holding up the derringer.

Exhausted, trying her best to breathe, Elizabeth realized she was completely helpless and quit fighting.

"That's better," the man said.

***

Leonard Newton could not believe his eyes or his luck. He had witnessed the capture of a woman on the trail below him and grinned with excitement. But then, on the upper trail he saw two riders walking their mounts. One of the walkers fell, and his horse ran away. Then came the report of a rifle. Using his spyglass, he saw his two kidnappers tie up another female.

"What in blazes?" questioned Leonard out loud. "Of all the luck, the fools captured both women!"

Thinking quickly, Leonard formed a plan.

One of them is undoubtedly Elizabeth. The other is that hired woman, what was her name? Blanche Graham. What to do next? The group on the lower trail will be to the cabin first. I'll get back there and be waiting.

Leonard ran down the hill and back to his horse. He mounted quickly and spurred the animal towards the nester's cabin. Coming to level ground, he pushed the horse to a gallop and continued at that pace. Riding for nearly fifteen minutes he made it to the cabin. Holding the shotgun he dismounted and checked the loads. Then, with his other hand, he pulled his Winchester .44-40 from its scabbard. Walking to the corner of the building, he leaned the weapons against the outside wall.

In ten minutes he heard riders. It was the two kidnappers from the lower trail with the hooded woman. Picking up the shotgun and hiding on the far side of the cabin, Leonard waited. The men rode up to the front of the building, halted their horses, and dismounted. The tied and hooded female remained seated on her mustang. Leonard appeared, took aim, and shot one man and then the other. One horse screamed and rode away. The other sidestepped at the blast of the shotgun but remained standing.

"What happened?" asked Blanche, still on her horse and frightened out of her wits. "What's happening?"

"No need to worry," lied Leonard, realizing this was not Elizabeth. "I shot your kidnappers. Come, slide left off the saddle and I'll help you down."

Blanche did as she was told, and Leonard caught her in his arms and helped her to her feet.

"I don't have time to untie you," said Leonard. "Come, I'll lead you inside a cabin and set you down. Others are coming."

Again, Blanche cooperated. Leonard led the woman into the cabin and set her on a chair. Running back outside, he went to a dead body, reached down, lifted it under the arms, and dragged it from the front of the cabin and around to the back.

He did this with the second kidnapper and then ran to catch the remaining horse. Leonard grabbed the reins, led the horse to the back, and tied it to a small cottonwood tree. Then he heard horses hooves pounding clearly from the west and coming nearer.

Leonard took his ambush spot near the side of the cabin. He picked up the rifle and waited. The man with the scar was leading Elizabeth's horse by the reins and the second kidnapper was following close behind. Leonard took aim and shot the first man in the right eye, just above his scar. The second outlaw, realizing he was in danger, reached for a pistol and, at the same time, spurred his horse and tried to gallop away. Leonard fired at the fleeing kidnapper and missed. The outlaw took aim and shot back. The pistol bullet burned Leonard's side, and too excited with the lust to kill, he barely felt it. He levered the Winchester, took aim, and shot the fleeing outlaw in the back. The hired killer fell slowly off of the galloping horse and was dead before he hit the ground.

"Who's there?" asked Elizabeth.

Given the circumstances, her voice was remarkably calm.

"Lizzy!" screamed Blanche, hearing her friend's voice.

"Blanche!" shouted Elizabeth. "Where are you?"

"I'm blindfolded and in a cabin."

Leonard levered another shell into his Winchester and, smiling ear to ear, went to the outlaw with the scar and made sure he was dead. Many yards further on, he came to the other fellow. Leonard prodded him with the barrel of the rifle, turned him over, and made sure he was not breathing.

"Well!" said Leonard Newton. "That turned out pretty good."

"Leonard?" asked Elizabeth, recognizing the distinct voice of her former acquaintance. "Leonard Newton?"

"Yes, Elizabeth Burnett," answered her former suitor. "It's me. Luckily, I came along and saved you from these terrible kidnappers. Who knows what could have happened."

Elizabeth, still up on her horse stiffened as her thoughts raced. She sat there, silent and unmoving.

"Lizzy!" screamed Blanche. "Please help me."

"Quiet, Blanche," replied Elizabeth. "I'm tied and blindfolded same as you. Save your strength and try to stay calm."

"All right," said Blanche. "I'll try, but I'm very afraid. I don't understand what is going on."

"Me either," replied Elizabeth.

"The same commanding Elizabeth Burnett," said Leonard. "Haven't changed at all, have you? Even when tied and blindfolded you have to get in the last word."

There was a long silence before she replied.

"What are you doing here, Leonard?" said the young woman. "You didn't have anything to do with this, did you?"

Another long silence.

"What do you think?"

"It couldn't be a coincidence," began Elizabeth. "Leonard, whatever you have in mind, give it up. Untie Blanche and me and let us go and I promise I will never implicate you. I'll give you money, if that's what you want. But let us go."

***

On the back trail, Larry Roth thought he heard a gunshot. It was very distant, and he stopped his horse to listen and then, hearing nothing further, continued on. He eventually came to the canyon and found Frank, the engineer, and Jack.

"Where's the boss and George?" asked Jack.

"I'm afraid I didn't wait for them," replied Larry.

"Why? What happened?"

"Blanche and I had a little disagreement, and I rode ahead."

"Frank and I were waiting for both of you. He has something to show you. Isn't that right, Frank?"

"Yes, but if your boss is not coming, I'm afraid we're wasting valuable time. You gave me a lot to do and…"

"It's my fault," replied Larry. "I'll ride back and…"

"We might as well ride together," said Jack.

The three men mounted and rode the trail eastward. Twenty minutes later they rode up on the dead body of George Temple. All three came to the instant realization that something had happened to Elizabeth.

"What do you think, Jack?" asked Larry.

"George was shot coming up the trail," said Jack, examining the marks on the ground. "Two men hid here and one of them pulled Elizabeth off her horse and dragged her. Then they put her back on her horse and rode off in that direction."

"I think the same thing," said Larry, also examining the tracks.

"The question is," said Jack. "What do we do next?"

"Two of us follow and one goes to town and gets word to the sheriff. When he's told, every man in the county will ride in the posse."

"You know that further up the trail they'll wipe out their tracks," said Jack.

"Time's wasting," said Larry. "Who goes for help, and who follows?"

"As much as I want to chase those hombre's," replied Jack. "I'm the one that knows the trails and shortcuts to Golden. I'll ride for help. You go after those dogs."

"Frank?" asked Larry.

"I'm an engineer, not a lawman," said Frank. "But I can shoot a rifle."

"Good," said Larry. "No help for it; we'll have to leave the body. Let's get to it."

The three men got back on their horses. Jack headed north while Frank and Larry began following the trail south.

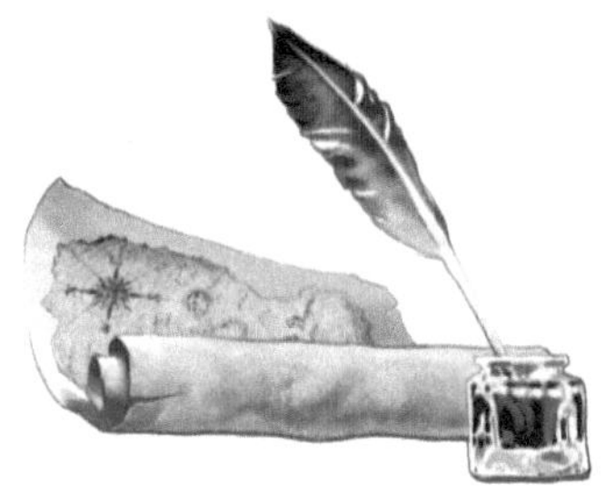

CHAPTER 26

Jack rode in on a lathered horse, and Rusty and Shorty were there to meet him.

"Elizabeth's been kidnapped!" shouted Jack.

Running to the corral, he lassoed a fresh horse and led him to a post. Switching tack, he wasted no time bridling and saddling the second mustang.

"Who done it?" asked Rusty.

"Don't know," replied Jack. "Larry and the engineer are following her trail."

"Jack," said Shorty. "Blanche is missing, too. She must have rode out right after you and Miss Elizabeth. Have you seen her?"

"No!" responded Jack. "What fools would kidnap our bosses? Don't they know they won't get away with it?"

"Maybe it's a crazy person," said Rusty.

"Two crazy persons?" said Jack. "Whoever did it will be dead by nightfall. I swear that. Rusty, rub down my hoss and gather the men. Be ready when I get back, and we'll form a posse for the sheriff."

"I'll load a wagon with food and supplies," interjected Shorty. "Men will need grub and coffee."

"Good thinking," said Jack. "Be ready, 'cause I'm gonna be movin' fast."

Jack jumped on the fresh horse and applied spurs, dust rising from flying hooves.

Pistol shots and a galloping mustang got people's attention along the main street of Golden, Colorado. From the Deputy Sheriff's Office, Chappy Blue came out on the boardwalk to see Jack ride a sweated horse to a stop in front of him.

"Miss Elizabeth and Miss Blanche are kidnapped!" shouted Jack. "I need men and help to follow and catch them that did this here thing."

"You heard the man!" shouted Chappy. "You're all deputized! Those that can, grab your horse and rifle and meet at the Double TJ Ranch!"

Men of all ages, from sixteen to eighty ran for weapons and a horse. Chappy sent someone to go to Denver to alert the sheriff, and within five minutes, a group of thirty men were following the deputy and Jack. Other men who took more time to find a weapon and a horse, came in scattered bunches. Within fifteen minutes word was traveling fast that the two ladies from the East were kidnapped and that a posse was gathering at their ranch. Within half an hour, more than a hundred men were riding to join the posse.

Shorty watched as Jack and Chappy rode in. Behind them, in scattered groups, came the posse. A wagon with horses hitched to it sat nearby with a supply of food and items for the trail. Rusty and the men from the Double TJ were standing nearby with horses saddled and ready. Each man had a rifle and a pistol.

“Men!” shouted Chappy Blue. “I deputize all of you! Listen! Jack and the hands from the Double TJ will follow me. We want to hurry but we don’t want to make so much noise that the kidnapper will harm or kill the women.

“I put Rusty in charge of the rest of you and all the others coming. Wait half an hour and then follow us. There aren’t many ways out of there. So when we find where the women are, I’ll send someone back to give you further instructions. Is that clear? Do exactly as I say, and don’t mess this up. Those girls’ lives depend on it.”

Chappy led his former ranch crew forward. When they got to George Temple’s body, the deputy left a crew member to stand guard against critters.

The men turned their horses and followed the tracks of the kidnappers and those by Lefty, Larry, and the engineer. Further on, the horse imprints disappeared over rocky ground, and the group of men dismounted and spread out. They walked forward, leading their horses, men examining the ground. It was Chappy who found the first faint imprint. The crew stayed on foot, leading their mounts. They stopped while the deputy and Jack worked out the trail. Again they mounted and rode behind Chappy as he followed hoofprints.

Coming to a rise, they saw a rider and stopped.

“Don’t shoot,” whispered Jack to the group. “It’s the engineer. His name is Frank.”

Frank saw the group, spurred his horse and hurried to meet them.

“Jack!” said Frank. “Larry and I followed the tracks. The kidnappers didn’t hide their trail very well. There’s a nester’s cabin about three miles from here. The last I saw, a man was dragging dead men and shoving them into a wash. Then he hid horses and went into the cabin. Larry stayed behind, and said he would get as close as possible. We didn’t see the women, but he thinks they’re inside.”

“What’ll we do, Chappy?” asked Jack.

“You men all know where that cabin is. We’ll ride close and hide the horses. No noise, no talking. Jack, you and I will try to find Larry and see what he knows. The rest of you men will surround the place and stay hidden.”

Taking no chances, Chappy halted the horses, a quarter mile from the building. The cowboys went in by foot, staying low and making no sound. They came out on a rise and spotted the cabin. The deputy signaled, and the Double TJ’s hands moved to surround the building. Chappy and Jack crept forward, looking to find Larry’s location. They moved to lower ground, keeping to cover behind cedar and pinion trees, and finally spotted Larry on the right side of the building. Larry was leaning against the wall and listening. Jack and Chappy joined him and they also put their ears to the cracked walls and listened too.

***

“Leonard,” said Elizabeth. “How do you expect to get away with this?”

The triumphant man let out a maniacal laugh. Blanche and Elizabeth, the coverings removed from their heads, looked at each other. Clearly this man was not in his right mind.

"I killed everyone involved, and no one knows where you are. Those men hid their tracks, and by the time they find you, it will be too late, and I'll be gone."

"Leonard," pleaded Elizabeth in a clear, calm voice. "I could give you money, and you could leave. We promise we will never tell anyone about you."

"Yeah, right," said Leonard, and then he laughed hysterically once again. "Just how much are you willing to give me for your freedom?"

"Five thousand dollars?" said Elizabeth, hesitating just a moment with her response.

"I've that much or more tucked away in my cabin. Is that all you think your life is worth?"

"That's all I brought with me," replied Elizabeth. "But I could get more. Say twenty-five thousand?"

"That's better. How would you get it to me?"

"I could wire my uncle. I could tell him that's what I need for the dams on the ranch, and he would send it."

"How do I know I can trust you?" asked Leonard, acting as if he was seriously considering her offer.

"I have never broken my word to anyone in my life," replied Elizabeth. "I won't start now. Leonard. If you let Blanche and me go, I promise to give you twenty-five thousand dollars and not tell anyone about this."

"Haven't changed a bit, have you, Elizabeth?" taunted Leonard. "The same haughty woman you've always been. Always in control."

"Will you accept my offer?" asked Elizabeth, hopefully.

"No."

"Why not, Leonard? This is the West; you don't really expect to get away with kidnapping us?"

"I do, and I have," laughed Leonard.

"What are you going to do with us?" Blanche asked, her voice quavering with fear.

"I never intended to have you involved," replied Leonard. "Those stupid fools I hired didn't have the brains to know the difference between you and Elizabeth. I'm afraid, my dear, that you've seen my face, and we can't have that."

"You're going to kill us?" asked Blanche.

"Just as soon as I teach Elizabeth that she can't treat me the way she did and get away with it. She's the first and only woman to reject me, and I swear… the very last."

Outside the three men clearly heard what the kidnapper said. To Chappy Blue, the peculiar man's voice sounded familiar. Peering through a crack, the deputy recognized the man from the barbershop. He remembered the fellow's cruelty and he realized the kidnapper was perfectly capable of harming the two women without conscience.

"You're a fool to harm us," said Elizabeth. "And you're deluding yourself if you think the men out here will let you get away with it."

Elizabeth was tied with hands behind her back, and so was Blanche. Leonard picked up a rope and doubled it around Blanche. She was still sitting unsecured. He tied one end of the rope around her and the chair, pulled it tight, and attached it to the leg of a heavy iron stove. Taking up another piece of rope, Leonard, took out a knife and began cutting lengths of it.

"Leonard," said Elizabeth. "Whatever you're thinking, don't do it."

"You know, my dearest Elizabeth, I've been planning this for a long time. I knew eventually I would get even. At first, I thought about holding you for ransom, but now I know I can get all the money I need. I bet you didn't know I was good at poker. And, if that fails, I can just steal it any time I want."

"What happened to you, Leonard? You have such a nice mother and father; how could you…"

"Shut up!" screamed Leonard. "Don't you ever mention them again!"

Leonard grabbed Elizabeth and shook her. Desperate, she stood up, despite her hands being tied behind her back and tried to run to the door. With a vice-like grip, Leonard grabbed her and dragged her back to the chair. He picked up the rope and tied it around her ankles. Then he brandished his opened pocket knife before the young woman.

Despite herself, Elizabeth's eyes widened, and for the first time in her life, she really felt fear.

"Leonard!" said Elizabeth. "Don't do this!"

"You leave Lizzy alone, you brute!" yelled Blanche.

"Shut up, both of you!" snarled Leonard.

The man placed the sharp blade across Elizabeth's cheek and gently pressed. Blood trickled from a small cut.

"Before I finish with you, Miss Rich and High and Mighty," exclaimed the crazed man, "you're going to wish you never said 'no' to me!"

Chappy and Larry rose from their positions and moved towards the front door. Jack, also rose and stepped to a window. All three men had their pistols cocked and ready. Listening for it, when Chappy and Larry busted against the door, Jack broke the window.

Leonard, confident no one knew of his location, had not barred the door. When it burst open, instead of grabbing for his sidearm, he pulled his derringer, from his vest pocket. Aiming at Chappy, he fired one barrel, and it hit the lawman in the upper left shoulder. Hearing the window burst, Leonard turned and shot Jack in the head, killing him instantly. Chappy and Larry, seeing Leonard was standing away from Elizabeth, opened fire and emptied five shots each into Leonard Newton. The thief, killer, and kidnapper was clearly shot to pieces and he fell to the floor.

Elizabeth, securely tied, sat there and watched the unfolding events with large, round eyes. Blanche had to turn her head and saw only part of the shootout.

"Larry!" Blanche screamed. "You saved us!"

"Chappy!" exclaimed Elizabeth, "you're shot!"

Crimson continued dripping from the deputy's wound. Chappy took a handkerchief from his pocket and tried to staunch the oozing flow of blood.

"Go see if that crazed idiot is dead, Larry," said Chappy, holding a hand over his dripping wound.

The thundering sound of horses' hooves and men shouting came loudly from outside. Apparently the orders Chappy Blue had given were not followed by the posse. Within a few moments, the front door was crowded. Many of the men were holding pistols. Larry cut Elizabeth's ropes and then Blanche's. Blanche flew into his arms, and Elizabeth went to Chappy, gently guided him to a kitchen chair, and sat him down. She took a white handkerchief from her pocket and pressed it on the dripping wound. She did her best to push and stop the flow.

Seeing that the kidnapper was dead, members of the posse dragged the body outside. Several hands of the Double TJ Ranch found Jack lying dead on the ground at the side of the house. Lefty went to the deputy in the cabin.

"Chappy," said Lefty. "That skunk killed Jack."

There came a roar of angry voices. Members of the posse picked up the body of the kidnapper and carried it to a single cottonwood on one side of the cabin. They threw up a rope around a high limb.

Placing a loop around the neck of the dead killer, men pulled and raised the body. The rope tied off, they left the kidnapper hanging by the neck and dangling in the wind, a warning for all outlaws.

Everyone was relieved that the women were rescued. Eventually, Shorty and his wagon arrived at the nester's cabin. Many of the posse, tired and hungry, cheered at the sight of the cook, and they helped unload the conveyance and set up a cooking pit and fire. Men's mouths wagged, as they were prone to do. And, while Shorty worked fixing food, he was told what had happened and that his friend Jack was dead.

"Gonna miss my pard," said Shorty in an angry voice. "Hangin' that feller ain't enough."

"Shorty," said Larry. "We need your wagon. We have to get Chappy Blue to the ranch and a doctor or he's not going to make it."

"Sure, you save that boy. I've got all the cookin' supplies I need. I'll stay and feed these fellers. Just make sure you send the wagon back."

Blankets were provided by the cook. The deputy was carried from the cabin to the bed of the wagon. Jack's body was wrapped and also placed in the back. Elizabeth asked Shorty for bandages and he gave her several clean towels. She climbed aboard and bandaged Chappy's wound as tightly as she could. The bleeding did not stop. They had to get to a doctor as quickly as possible. With Blanche sitting up front, Larry took the reins and drove the wagon towards the ranch. Lefty volunteered to ride for the sawbones. Chappy was losing a lot of blood and he lay semiconscious and fighting for his life. Men watched as the wagon drove away.

Left behind, Shorty set two giant kettles to boiling beans and several coffee pots to fire while he began mixing dough for biscuits. A steer had the misfortune to come near, and someone from the posse shot it and men moved in to carve it up. Steaks began to fry and pieces of cooked meat ended up in the bean pot. Some of the posse returned to town disappointed that the chase had ended so quickly. But the majority stayed to enjoy the special day and to celebrate that Miss Blanche and Miss Elizabeth were saved.

Everyone knew Shorty's reputation as a cook, and some men using borrowed utensils and others having their own helped themselves to biscuits, beans, and cooked meat. As in all posses, bottles were brought and collected at the end of a makeshift table of boards. Coffee cups were liberally dosed with alcohol. The day passed, and darkness came, and some fellows became quite mellow. The men talked and laughed about the day's events and then someone got the idea of setting fire to the nester's cabin. The blaze illuminated the night, created great warmth, and burned for a long time. Eventually, bedrolls came out, and under a clear star-studded night, some men slept while others kept a fire going and ate the last of the food and drank the last of the liquor and coffee.

In the morning, the festivities were over. Shorty, out of supplies, waited for the wagon to return and to hear about Chappy Blue's condition. Members of the posse departed in sporadic groups. At midmorning, the wagon returned with Lefty driving.

"How's Chappy?" asked Shorty.

"The doctor operated and took out the bullet, but he lost a lot of blood. Doc says it don't look good."

The last of the posse, some twenty men, hearing the bad news waited for the cook. Shorty and several hands from the Double TJ Ranch packed up the cooking supplies and headed back. Lefty had brought his horse, and mounting, he made a suggestion.

"The main herd has been left unguarded these last twenty-four hours. How about if Rusty and I head that way?"

"Probably should have left at least one man with the herd," said Shorty.

"Cookie," replied Rusty. "You know that no hand would be left out of the search."

The cook slapped reins, and the chuckwagon followed its previous tracks back towards the ranch. Twenty minutes passed and the last of the group heard distant rifle shots.

"Could be rustlers," said the cook.

The last of the posse, still hoping for excitement and a purpose, turned their horses in the direction of the gunfire. Shorty, on his wagon, unable to follow, headed back to the ranch.

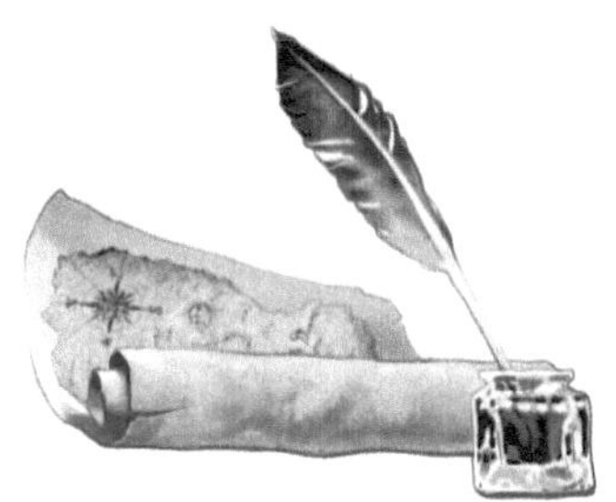

CHAPTER 27

"I tell you," said Jacob. "The herd at the Double TJ Ranch will be totally unguarded. All the ranch hands are chasing that fool kidnapper and the men he hired."

"What about the posse?" asked one of his fellow rustlers. "What if we run into them?"

"They're looking for those two women, not us," replied Jake. "If we run into them, we can pretend to join them."

Jacob and his men rose early in the morning, came across Double TJ land, and encountered no living man. They skirted the ranch house and buildings and they looked deserted. The outlaw leader was right; the ranch hands were chasing the kidnappers along with the posse. Heading northwest Jacob and five of his men ran into the unguarded herd. They cut out twelve large steers and headed directly south to a trail they had used many previous times. Once they reached the hills, they would travel over rocky ground and take the cattle along a path only the rustlers knew. Miles south, far from the Double TJ Ranch, they would rebrand the stock and take them to a meat buyer who bought such animals.

Lefty and Rusty came over a rise of ground and saw six men pushing twelve steers.

"Rustlers!" whispered Rusty.

Pulling rifles, the two men tied their horses and found shelter. They needed to cut the men off before they came to the mountains and the edge of the ranch property.

"This must be where they've been taking the stolen cattle," said Rusty. "Look, between those two hills, the ground is solid granite. No wonder we never found their trail."

The six men and twelve steers were coming directly towards them. Lefty fired first, and it was Jacob, the leader, who took a bullet in the heart and died before hitting the ground. Rusty, aimed his rifle at a second man and missed. Then, the five rustlers turned their horses in unison, abandoned the steers, and rode straight west.

Lefty and Rusty continued to fire their rifles until the rustlers disappeared into low ground. Running back to their horses, they mounted and followed. The thieves were good at avoiding capture, and once again, they were making a successful escape. The difference this day was that sporadic remnants of the posse were spread across the Double TJ Ranch. Running at full speed, the rustlers came up on a group of men who looked down on them from a steep slope. The outlaws turned and headed east to avoid this group.

The posse, unsure of what was happening, did not fire on the rustlers. Then Lefty and Rusty broke from the brush, saw the men on the crest, and shouted, “RUSTLERS”! From above, rifles were drawn and over fifteen posse members began shooting at the fleeing outlaws. Hearing the continuing gunfire, others from the posse across the ranch turned their horses back toward the sound. Soon, the rustlers found themselves in a gauntlet of men coming from many directions. Most of the posse saw the fleeing rustlers but did not fire; it was unclear what was happening. Lefty and Rusty continued pursuit and when seeing other men, again shouted, “RUSTLERS!”

Then, the years of luck finally ran out for the thieves. Thirsty for action, various members of the posse fired at the fleeing outlaws. A barrage of bullets cut down the five remaining rustlers, including their horses.

CHAPTER 28

Nerves frayed almost beyond endurance, Elizabeth sought a cup of coffee from the cook shack. In Shorty's absence, Blanche had prepared coffee for Larry and her employer. Elizabeth left the two at a table, took her cup, and paced the courtyard.

For hours Elizabeth stayed close to Chappy Blue. She had held her hand tightly against the wound on his chest trying to stop the bleeding without success. Towards the end, she began to believe he would die. No human could lose so much blood and survive. The bullet must have nicked a vein.

When the doctor came she refused to leave Chappy. She assisted Larry and Blanche while he called for more lamps, alcohol, and bandages. The doctor removed the bullet. It was such a small piece of lead to cause so much damage.

"Good thing it was a Derringer," said the doctor. "Anything larger would have killed him."

When the operation was over, the bleeding stopped, and he was properly bandaged, Elizabeth asked.

"Will he live, doctor?"

"I don't know. He's lost a lot of blood. The next twenty-four hours should tell."

Elizabeth begged the doctor to stay but he refused.

"I have two babies to deliver and both are ten miles apart. As soon as that's over, I'll return."

"Doctor, no one knows, but I am a very rich woman. I'll pay you anything you ask if you will stay."

"It doesn't matter," responded the physician, "I still have to go. Besides, Miss Elizabeth, there's nothing more I can do here. All that will help now is prayer and to keep him cool and comfortable."

Elizabeth returned to his room and watched over the wounded man.

Please, God, please let him live. I'll do anything you wish; just let him live.

As the day passed, Elizabeth repeated these words over and over, hour after hour.

Blanche came to tell Elizabeth that Shorty had returned with the wagon, but she was too intent upon Chappy and his condition to pay much attention. Shorty brought her food and more coffee. Elizabeth drank but refused to eat. She heard whispered conversation outside the bedroom door where Blanche and Larry were talking.

"I am afraid she is making herself ill," Blanche said to Larry. "I don't dare tell her I'm leaving until we find out what happens to Chappy."

"I hate it, honey," said Larry, "but I know you're right."

A day later, the doctor returned and examined the wounded man. His response to Elizabeth's questions was to shake his head. The exhausted doctor agreed to stay and was given George Temple's bed to sleep in. Elizabeth continued to sit in the chair next to Chappy. Hours passed. She applied cool, fresh cloths to his fevered forehead and waited. Night came, and as he lay in bed, Elizabeth reached out. She kept a hand on his shoulder and slept in fits.

Sometime in the night, the fevered Chappy called out, and Lizzy awoke.

"Elizabeth won't care for a man like me!" he murmured.

"Oh yes, I will," she responded.

She touched his forehead and it was burning up with fever. She took a cloth from a bowl of water, rung it out, and began wiping sweat from his body.

"No fancy lady for Chappy!" shouted the delirious man.

"Chappy!" said Elizabeth. "I'm here!"

"Can't have no lady be the boss!" mumbled the sick man.

Chappy suddenly jerked and tried to sit up. Frantically and with all her strength, Elizabeth pushed him down and screamed for help.

"Doctor! Larry! Blanche!"

"Always giving orders!" replied Chappy.

The doctor came into the room.

"What's the trouble?" he asked.

"He's in a terrible fever," said Elizabeth, "talking out of his mind and trying to sit up."

"You hold him down," said the doctor, putting a hand on his patient's forehead. "He's burning up, all right."

The doctor picked up a pan of fresh water and poured it over Chappy's hair, wetting the fevered man down. Taking a bottle of diluted vinegar, the physician removed sheets off the patient, took up a cloth and poured the liquid on it. Then he rubbed the vinegar over Chappy's chest and arms. The man struggled, and Elizabeth did her best to hold him down.

"You're doing good, Miss Elizabeth," said the doc. "Don't let him open that wound."

The vinegar seemed to have an effect and Chappy quit struggling.

"Pretty lady, though," mumbled Chappy. "Lizzy is sure a pretty lady."

"Seems he's talking about you," smiled the doctor.

Lizzy felt her face redden.

"He seems to be getting worse," cried Elizabeth. "What can we do?"

"I'd say he's fighting it. This fever breaks and I'll bet he recovers. You go get some more fresh water to cool him. Ask Blanche and Larry to come watch him. If you're not going to leave him, at least you can get some sleep."

"No!" said Elizabeth. "I won't leave!"

"Do as I say!" ordered the doctor.

The young woman did as she was told and returned with Larry, Blanche, and a basin of water.

"This girl's exhausted," said the doc.

Just as the physician spoke, Elizabeth, hours without sleep and pushed to her limit, went limp. Larry caught her, lifted her, and placed her in the chair next to Chappy. Her head rested on the bed against the sick man's shoulder. Only a few seconds before, Chappy had been squirming. As soon as Lizzy's face touched his shoulder, he quieted.

"Miss Elizabeth," said the delirious Chappy, and then he smiled.

Blanche picked up a cloth and began wiping the sick man's forehead.

"That's it," said the doctor. "Keep him cool. Use the vinegar rub every once in a while. I'm going next door and try to catch up on my sleep. But it looks like the lady next to him might be the cure. Leave her there."

The doctor pleased with himself, smiled and left the room.

Larry and Blanche stayed and watched over both of them. From time to time Blanche applied cool compresses to Chappy's forehead. And then early in the morning, the fever seemed to break. Larry and Blanche left the room to get a cup of coffee and a short breath of fresh air. A few moments after that, Chappy opened his eyes, fully conscious. He felt warmth beside him and instinctively knew who it was. He turned and saw the top of her head and the side of her face. Even in exhausted sleep, she was beautiful.

He lay like that for some minutes, observing her. Elizabeth awakened, her eyes opened, and she immediately came to her feet. Holding the bedpost, the young woman put one hand on Chappy's chest and looked down.

"Well," said Chappy. "If I knew you liked me this much, I would have told you how I felt."

"And what is that?" asked Lizzy in a strange quakey voice.

"That I love you, Miss Elizabeth, even if you are a pain and full of yourself."

Lizzy smiled.

"Why Chappy," she said, continuing to gently touch his warm chest, "I feel exactly the same way about you."

In obvious discomfort, he reached up, took hold of her arm and pulled. Lizzy, understanding, bent down and kissed him on the lips. The kiss was long and warm—and when they finally parted, Elizabeth willingly surrendered her heart.

ABOUT THE AUTHOR

Charlie Steel is a novelist and internationally published short story writer.

Steel, author of **Desert Heat, Desert Cold and Other Tales of the West,** and other novels and anthologies, has worked in assorted occupations starting at the age of ten. Some of his experiences include service in the Army, laborer in the oil fields, construction, foundry worker, and salvage diver. Early in his life, he was recruited by the US Government and spent seven years behind the Iron Curtain. His undercover assignments monitored Russian activity.

Steel attended eight universities and currently holds five degrees, including a PhD.

Charlie Steel is an avid traveler, hunter and fisherman. He lives on an isolated ranch at the base of Greenhorn Mountain in Southern Colorado. (www.charliesteel.net)

ABOUT THE ILLUSTRATOR

Illustrator Barabash Sviatoslav was born in the city of Kovel, Ukraine. At sixteen, he became interested in drawing. For fourteen years he continued his studies as an artist/ painter. He attended and graduated from the Odessa Art College and the National Academy of Painting in Kyiv. Sviatoslav, a member of the Union of Artists, has participated in exhibitions of the Union of Artists of Ukraine and his own personal events.

Sviatoslav credits his grandfather, Alexander Manelyuk, a graphic designer, as being his first teacher. His grandfather taught him to appreciate the beauty of nature, especially landscapes with their endless varieties.

Among other art projects, Sviatoslav is currently illustrating books. Lately, he has become interested in digital art with its endless possibilities.

Dear Reader,

If you enjoyed reading **TWO WOMEN CONQUER THE WEST (AND THEIR HEARTS)** please help promote the book by posting a review on Amazon.com and following Charlie Steel on social media.

https://www.facebook.com/CharlieSteelAuthor
https://www.goodreads.com/author/show/3484434.Charlie_Steel

Charlie Steel can also be contacted at charliesteel.usa@gmail.com or by writing to the following address:

Charlie Steel
c/o Condor Publishing, Inc.
PO Box 39
Lincoln, Michigan 48742

Warm greetings
G. Heath, publisher

www.ingramcontent.com/pod-product-compliance
Lightning Source LLC
Chambersburg PA
CBHW030356310726
48979CB00001B/327

* 9 7 8 1 9 3 1 0 7 9 6 6 2 *